Praise for Shelli Stevens' *Dangerous Grounds*

Rating: 5 Angels and a Recommended Read "With suspense, humor and sex, Dangerous Grounds is an enthralling read, with enough depth of emotion, heat and tension to engross anyone.... With a voice and style all her own, Ms. Stevens has yet again proven her worth with Dangerous Grounds..."

~ *Rachel C, Fallen Angel Reviews*

Rating: 5 Ribbons "Blended seamlessly the action and sexual chemistry jump off the pages of DANGEOUS GROUNDS and make Ms. Stevens' latest novel a recommended read."

~ *Romance Junkies*

"Shelli Steven's Dangerous Grounds is one sexy read! ...Wonderful sexual tension, witty dialog and a well written suspense backstory team up to give readers a thrilling ride."

~ *Lauren Dane, Author of Samhain's Chase Brothers Series*

Rating: 5 Flags "...The suspense, mystery and holy smokes—the heat between Gabe and Madison would cause spontaneous combustion without flicking an eyelash... Dangerous Grounds has become the latest keeper in Shelli's works as far as I'm concerned."

~ *Melisa, Euro Reviews*

Rating: 5 Nymphs "Dangerous Games is another great story by author Shelli Stevens, so I'll say up front that I loved it. The storyline is fast paced, and it's filled with passion, sizzling hot sex, suspense, danger and a little intrigue ...I eagerly await the next addition to the Seattle Steam series, Tempting Adam."

~ *Literary Nymphs*

Look for these titles by
Shelli Stevens

Now Available:

Trust and Dare

The Seattle Steam Series:
Dangerous Grounds
Tempting Adam

Dangerous Grounds

Shelli Stevens

A SAMHAIN PUBLISHING, LTD. publication.

Samhain Publishing, Ltd.
577 Mulberry Street, Suite 1520
Macon, GA 31201
www.samhainpublishing.com

Dangerous Grounds
Copyright © 2008 by Shelli Stevens
Print ISBN: 978-1-59998-992-1
Digital ISBN: 1-59998-850-X

Editing by Laurie M. Rauch
Cover by Dawn Seewer

First Samhain Publishing, Ltd. electronic publication: January 2008
First Samhain Publishing, Ltd. print publication: November 2008

Dedication

Thank you to Cherry Adair for being such a wonderful mentor and hero. For the selfless giving and inspiration you've bestowed on many, but most of all on me. You truly are amazing. Not to mention funny as hell.

Thank you to my family and friends, to my very first critique group (Heather and Lisa), to Robin Rotham, to my fabulous beta readers Jo and Danielle, to my Naughty and Spice blog sisters Lillian Feisty, Karen Erickson, and Amie Stuart, to GSRWA, to Lauren Dane for the wonderful cover quote, and finally to my editor, Laurie M. Rauch. All of you made this book possible.

Chapter One

That settled it. The next person to ask why she had come to the party alone was getting the bowl of guacamole thrown at them.

Madison Phillips squeezed her hand around a diet soda, crushing the can and raising the level of the cola. Taking a deep breath, she looked at her brother, who stood below a banner proclaiming, "Welcome home, Eric!"

Her scowl deepened. Not because Eric had returned home from fighting in Iraq—she was more than proud of that. No, it was because he had his beautiful girlfriend snuggled under his arm. They looked so in love it made her nauseous. There were at least a dozen of them—happy couples spread about and looking like they couldn't wait to get back to the bedroom.

Being the only person without a date, she felt like the damn black sheep of the room. She felt ridiculously self-conscious. But more than that, she felt alone.

"Hi, Madison. Isn't it great to have your brother home?" Her cousin Stacia passed the refreshment table and grabbed a chip, stuffing it in her mouth. "Hey, where's Bradley?"

Madison glanced at the bowl of guacamole. *Hmm. If I dumped it on her pink cashmere sweater, she'd look kind of like a watermelon.* She glanced back up, forcing a polite smile onto her face as she shrugged.

"We're no longer together."

"What?" Her cousin's jaw dropped, her voice rising with unnecessary drama. She leaned forward and stage whispered, "Was it a mutual thing?"

Madison sighed. "No, Stacia. It wasn't a mutual thing. He broke up with me."

"Really? The bastard! He should've put a ring on your finger a long time ago."

Madison blinked, her stomach clenching at the fact her cousin had brought up such an awkward subject in a room full of people.

Most of the people in the room had turned toward them, their expressions ones of sympathy. *I'm not related to this woman. It's impossible.* Stacia must have been the result of an extramarital affair.

"And aren't you tactful." She didn't have the energy to be polite anymore, but winced as the words left her mouth. "I'm sorry. Excuse me, I just need some air."

She walked away before she could say anything else bitchy.

Seeing all those couples had also brought up some other feelings. The realization at just how long she'd gone without sex. Though Bradley had just dumped her two days ago, they hadn't done the wild thing since Valentine's Day. Four months without getting laid should be considered a crime. Talk about a constant state of horniness.

"Hey, kid." Eric caught her just before she stepped outside. "Thanks for the party."

Her annoyance faded, replaced by a warm affection for her brother. Ignoring the kid label, she murmured, "It's the least we could do."

"Did you behave yourself while I was gone? Not doing

anything too dangerous or crazy, are you?"

Even after just returning from a war zone, her brother's concerns were about her. He was so damn protective. Always had been.

She lifted an eyebrow. "I'm always on my best behavior, remember?"

"Wait, are we talking about the same Madison Phillips?" He tweaked a strand of her hair. "I worry about you, kid."

"I know you do. And it's very sweet. Have you made the rounds socializing with all the relatives?"

"Most of them. I've been avoiding Stacia, though. Never could handle her."

Her lips twitched into a smile. "Yeah, good call on that one."

"Well. I guess I'd better get back to the party. Be inside in about an hour, okay? I've got a surprise."

"All right, have fun." She gave him a quick hug, and slipped outside onto the balcony.

She rested her arms on the stone railing and stared out into the night, taking a moment to consider her new status as a single woman. She needed to move on, and fast. What was that saying? The best way to get over someone was to get under someone else. Easier said than done, though.

Her thoughts were momentarily distracted by the view in front of her. She'd never get used to it. Her parents' home sat atop Queen Anne Hill and looked out over the Seattle skyline. Tonight the buildings twinkled through a clear night, and the Space Needle seemed close enough to touch.

She sighed and inhaled the warm spring air. Her mind turned back to the idea of meeting a man just for fun. Rebound sex. Hmm, not a bad idea, but could she actually do it? Having casual sex had never been her thing.

Though it was inevitable that the next person she tried to sleep with would pretty much just turn out to be the transition guy. Why not choose the time and the man, and get it over with? She could find someone available, attractive, and with no strings attached. Besides, getting laid would be good for her.

Images flitted through her head. Images of a man's weight pinning her to the bed while he moved deep inside her. Her sex clenched, wanting something to fill the constant ache.

"You know...I think I'm gonna do it," she muttered aloud.

"Do what?"

She spun from the railing, her eyes widening with surprise as she made out the shape of a man half-hidden in the shadows. He stepped forward into the light and her breath caught.

Thank you, God. Whoever had coined the expression *tall, dark, and handsome* must've meant this man. His eyes were a dark coffee brown, the expression in them closed off and unreadable. He had short hair, just darker than his eyes. Even if the trace of accent hadn't colored his voice, his features gave away his Latino heritage. And the body? He had Bradley beat hands down.

Her body, already jacked up from the possibility of having sex, grew warm and tingly.

"Are you done?"

Madison's gaze snapped back up to meet his. Done? She hadn't even gotten started.

If she planned on going through with this, then he had to be her man. Gabriel Martinez—her brother's best friend. Her mind compared the Gabe from several years ago to the Gabe now standing in front of her. He was, without a doubt, a sex god. A sex god who would be her rebound. Well, if he could be persuaded.

"Am I done?" She licked her lips. "What do you mean?"

"Giving me a visual inspection."

His voice ran deep, with the slightest bit of abrasiveness to it. You knew right away this was a man you didn't want to piss off. Good thing he sounded somewhat amused.

"Well, now." She stepped forward and tilted her head, giving him a small smile. "What if I said that you require closer inspection?"

"Nice." He shook his head and then smiled. "Were you always this much of a flirt, Maddie?"

"Sorry, Gabe. I haven't seen you in a while and am just discovering that being a cop has been good to you." Her gaze drifted down his body again. Tall, muscular, hard. "Very good to you."

He had to have noticed her sexual undertones, but he ignored them and took a drink of the soda in his hand instead.

Doubt pricked at her. Was she way out of her league? He hadn't checked her out once. Madison crossed her arms, feeling a bit self-conscious. It wasn't like she was bad looking. She kept her long brown hair in a trendy cut, adding highlights to bring out the golden flecks in her hazel eyes. Her toned body was the result of several hours a week of spinning classes and strippercize.

She was twenty-five, Gabe six years older than she. It wasn't a tremendous age gap, but in her teen years it had meant that their social circles never crossed. She'd had a crush on him when he'd first moved up to Seattle, but the adoration had ended when he began sporting facial hair and listening to Nirvana.

"Well, I'd better get back inside. Nice to see you again, Maddie." Gabe stepped toward the door.

Tell him to stop, she ordered herself. *Ask him out to dinner.*

"Nobody calls me Maddie anymore." She winced. Okay, totally blew that one.

"Ah." He gave a humorless smile and opened the sliding glass door to the house. He sounded almost disappointed when he murmured, "You sure have grown up, haven't you?"

He had no idea. Madison darted forward in her Gucci heels, trying not to trip as she intercepted him at the door. She slammed her hand against the glass, blocking his escape.

"I don't know if Eric told you," she began with a sultry smile. "But I'm opening up my own espresso shop. The grand opening is Monday morning."

His eyes held the faintest flicker of surprise. "Really? Who would have guessed...Maddie Phillips, the newest coffee entrepreneur."

"Madison. I know, isn't it great?" She laughed. Her gaze dropped from Gabe's bemused eyes to the hard chest outlined through his Seahawks T-shirt. Swallowing hard as she felt a sudden pressure between her legs, she tore her gaze away and fumbled in her purse for a business card and pen.

She scrawled a hurried note on it and handed it to him. "Here's my card. I've written you a coupon for a free drink. I'll be getting things set up all weekend, so if you drop by I can make you a practice mocha."

"Ooo La Latté. Nice name." He glanced up from the card and started to hand it back to her. "I'm not big on coffee—"

"We also have tea," she interrupted, a little more forcefully than necessary. "And hot chocolate. In any case, it's a free beverage. How can you pass that up?"

He remained quiet for a moment and then nodded. "You're right, I can't. I'll see if I can drop by."

He tucked the card into the back pocket of his jeans. She had to fight the ridiculous urge to ask him to turn around so that she could get a view of his backside.

"I'm going to need a faithful customer base, so you'd better visit me often." She placed a hand on his arm and felt the bulge of his biceps. This man was built.

The image she'd had earlier of a man on top of her altered slightly. The man had a face now and it was Gabe's. Her nipples hardened and she swallowed with difficulty.

This time she didn't miss the flicker of sexual awareness in his gaze, and her pulse sped up.

"After all," she continued, her voice husky. "You've got to support your best friend's little sister."

His eyes narrowed and she knew she'd made a mistake. *Great, Madison.* She ground her teeth together. *Remind him that you're Eric's little sister. That's sure to have him jumping your bones. Time to make an exit—get out of here so it's not so obvious. And leave him with a nice parting view, of course.*

"I'm going to grab some of that crab quiche. So yummy! See you this weekend, Gabe." She slid past him, making sure her hip brushed his thigh as she opened the door and went back into the house.

Gabe watched as Madison stepped inside the house, her hips swinging provocatively. He fisted his hands, determined to not act on his primal desire to reach out and smack her ass. But, God, what a nice ass it was, even in those wide-leg pants that women wore nowadays. He shook his head and tried to stop the thoughts that were going where they pretty much shouldn't go.

No way was he getting into bed with Eric's little sister. No matter how nice her ass, or how voluptuous her breasts. Breasts that had been just about falling out of that satiny little top under her blazer.

Enough. Gabe shook his head. *If you need to get laid, there are plenty of willing women out there.* Like Danica down at the station. His mind conjured up the image of the tall redhead and her enormous mouth that put a man's imagination to work. The secretary had made it clear that she'd like to try him on in the bedroom. But even if he had been interested—which he wasn't—she'd already slept with half the cops in his precinct.

His gaze drifted through the door and he spotted Maddie speaking to her dad. She glanced over at the patio. Even though he knew she couldn't see him past the reflection of the glass inside, she raised an eyebrow and her mouth curved into a slow smile.

Gabe's erection strained against his jeans and he cursed the unwanted reaction. She'd never shown any interest in him before, so why now? Well, maybe when she had been a kid. She'd followed him around for a few years after he'd first moved up here, but that had been an adolescent crush.

They hadn't seen each other in years. She'd gone on a trip to Europe after graduating high school, funded by mommy and daddy. It seemed she'd loved Italy so much that she'd decided to stay for a year and work at some café.

Eric had always adored his sister, and would brag about how Maddie knew what she wanted out of life and made sure she got it.

Gabe agreed with that theory, although taking a somewhat different point of view on how she got it. The girl was flat-out spoiled. Her first car had been a Lexus. When she'd wanted a dog, her parents had one bred for her from a Best in Show winner. And, according to Eric, her prom dress had cost more than some wedding dresses. The fact that she'd gone back to school to get an MBA surprised him, but everything up to that point, and even after, still remained the same.

And now she was back in Seattle. He hadn't even seen her in about six years. Six years ago she'd just been Eric's little sister. Six years ago she hadn't had those breasts. Now she looked and acted like every man's wet dream.

He shook his head. No way was he going to her espresso shop this weekend. It was clear she was offering more than just coffee. He might as well tear up the card now.

The sliding door opened and Eric stepped out.

"What's going on?" Eric came to stand next to him on the balcony. "I saw you catching up with Madison."

"Yeah." Gabe forced a smile. Were his thoughts written all over his face? The dirty ones running rampant in his head about Maddie? The ones Eric would probably be happy to knock him out over if he knew about them? "I guess she doesn't like to be called Maddie anymore."

Eric laughed and took a swig of his beer. "No, she doesn't. My little sister has grown into a sophisticated lady."

Hmm, and it seemed the sophisticated lady was trying to seduce a cop. Wouldn't be the first time. But it couldn't happen with Maddie. No matter how fuckable she looked, she was still Eric's little sister. He could fantasize all he wanted, but the erection stopped there.

"Are you glad to be back?" he asked, trying to clear his thoughts. "I hear Iraq is a bitch."

Eric shook his head and his smile fell. "It was intense. I haven't decided whether I'll re-enlist next year."

"You don't have to. Four years as an officer in the army

17

looks pretty good when you're running for Senate."

"That isn't why I joined." Eric gave him a pointed look.

"I know." Gabe thrust his hands into the pockets of his jeans. "Sorry. That was uncalled for."

"It's cool." Eric paused. "Hey, I'm going to propose to Lannie tonight after the party. I'd like you to be my best man in our wedding."

"Congratulations. I'd be honored."

He wasn't at all surprised at Eric's news. Eric was the type who wanted to settle down and have kids. To be a loving husband and father, and buy a mansion in Bellevue. Then become a state senator, just like his grandpa had been.

Eric wanted everything that Gabe didn't.

"Thanks...what about you, Gabe? Anyone special on the sideline?"

"God, no." Gabe gave a humorless smile. "Just the occasional fuck here and there."

Eric winced. "It doesn't have to be like that. Maybe if you—"

"No, it does." He sighed. "I'm not trying to be a dick, Eric. But you know me. You know my past, and what I've been through. And you know that's exactly what it has to be like for me."

Eric stayed silent for a moment, then answered with a quiet, "I'm going to have to disagree. I think you need to stop blaming yourself for something that wasn't your fault. You'll meet someone someday, and it'll all change."

"I doubt it," Gabe replied. "Now enough already. This is your day of celebration. You don't want to spend your second day back in America arguing about my shitty dating life." He headed toward the door. "I'm hungry. Didn't you say your parents were serving some kind of fancy dinner?"

"Salmon with lemon caper sauce." Eric followed him inside.

"What the hell is a caper?"

"I think it's some kind of vegetable. But it sounds damn good. You don't want to know the kind of stuff I was eating in Iraq."

"You're right." Gabe laughed, knowing the tension had passed. "I don't want to know."

℘

Madison finished arranging the ceramic mugs on a shelf and stood back to admire her work. Besides running a standard espresso shop, she also planned to sell local artwork and pottery. She loved the idea of supporting local artists and having something besides espresso to offer.

She glanced around the shop. It was clean, stocked, and ready for the grand opening tomorrow morning. Everything looked amazing, if she did say so herself.

The shiny black tiles of the floor contrasted with the walls, which were painted a soft jade green. The marble countertops were lined with coffee accessories, along with tulip-filled vases.

And she loved the tables. French-café-inspired, they were glass with black rimming. The chairs had heart-shaped backs, with the same black steel construction as the tables, and soft leather seats.

The leather couch and matching chairs had been a great investment, encouraging those who wanted to linger, perhaps read a book or a magazine, and maybe even buy a second mocha.

Now all I have to do is draw in business. That shouldn't be too hard—she'd arranged to have a dollar-off coupon run in the

Seattle Times with an announcement of her grand opening.

Madison glanced at the clock hanging on the wall, an Art Deco antique that she'd paid way too much for but looked fabulous in her shop.

Her heart sank and she lowered her gaze. Seven already. She'd stayed all day yesterday and too long today as it was. Gabe wasn't going to show, she might as well admit it.

What a disappointment, because she'd made a point of looking ultra-sexy today. Low-rise jeans showed off her tiny pink thong, if she happened to bend over, and a clingy black T-shirt that read *They're Real* hugged her breasts.

Okay, maybe it was a little on the flirty or suggestive side. But she really wanted this to happen with Gabe. So the word discretion was just going to have to be eliminated from her vocabulary.

She moved toward the door and yelped when a figure stepped up to the glass. Her shoulders relaxed. It was just Gabe. Her stomach dipped with nerves as she realized what that meant. Gabe was actually here. He'd shown up.

He gave a light tap on the window and gestured for her to unlock the door.

Nice, Madison, stare at him through a locked door and look like an idiot. She fumbled with the lock on the door and swung it inward.

"Hey there." She smiled, glancing up at him from under her lashes. "I didn't think you were going to show this weekend. Welcome to my little coffee shop."

Gabe seemed to hesitate before he stepped across the threshold. "This is a nice part of Seattle for you to set up business in." He glanced around. "It looks great. How did you afford it?"

"Part loan, part parents," Madison replied, a bit breathless. He looked even better tonight than he had on Friday. He was such a jeans and T-shirt guy, she decided as he walked past her. And his ass was just as nice as she'd assumed it would be. Yes, seducing him would be all too enjoyable.

"I picked the location because it's more residential, meaning more parking. I want my customers to linger. Plus, I'm in the same plaza as a day spa. I know that'll be good for business." She took in a rapid, nervous breath. "I can't tell you how many times I get done having a facial and all I want is a latté."

Gabe gave her an *I'll take your word on it* expression and settled down in one of the chairs at a table.

"Have you hired any employees?"

Madison sat across from him. "Sarah. She's been a barista with Starbucks for three years. I offered her a five-dollar raise if she quit and came to work for me. She's in college and could seriously use the extra cash, so of course she took it. She's a goddess at making espresso drinks."

"Along with you, right?"

"No, umm, not so much." She waved her hand through the air in dismissal. "Until yesterday I'd never made a latté in my life. Hell, I could barely make a pot of coffee."

He blinked, seeming stunned by the news. "You don't know how to make espresso? And you're opening your own business?"

"Will you please give me some credit, Gabe?" She rolled her eyes. "I've downed a ton of the stuff."

"Are you kidding me?"

"No. Look, I worked at that café in Italy for a year. I saw them doing it—I just never did it myself." She gave an impatient

21

sigh and stood. "I know what you're thinking, but you're wrong. The people I'm leasing the espresso equipment from gave me lessons and I'll make coffee when I need to. But that's why I hired Sarah. She's my barista. I'm just managing things and working the cash register for now."

"Yeah..."

"There's money in coffee, Gabe. The latté I charge almost three dollars for only costs me forty-five cents. Cup included." She leaned over him and whispered, "Trust me. I know exactly what I'm doing."

His eyes met hers and she caught her breath. It looked like coffee was the last thing on his mind. His gaze dropped to her breasts, which were at his eye level, and her nipples tightened in anticipation.

"Nice."

Her pulse raced as heat shot straight between her legs. Was he talking about her breasts? But his comment sounded amused.

Madison looked down at her chest and flushed. Of course. How could she have forgotten what her shirt said? So maybe it wasn't the breasts he'd been checking out. Bummer.

She jerked back and hurried around the counter to the espresso equipment. "You left the party early on Friday night. Did you hear that Eric and Lannie got engaged?"

"Yeah." His gaze followed her. "Eric told me earlier in the night he was planning on popping the question. Do they have a date yet?"

"Are you kidding?" Madison started preparing his mocha. "By the end of the night she'd picked a date, a caterer, and a location."

"Hmm. I guess she wasn't too surprised by the proposal

either."

"Yeah, not so much. I'm sure she's already picked out the names of their future children." Madison grated a bit of a chocolate bar on top of the drink and carried it out to him. "Lannie asked me to be a bridesmaid. I think it's a pity position just because I'm Eric's sister. God knows she has enough friends."

"I'm the best man." Gabe stared down at the drink that she'd placed in front of him. "Is this coffee?"

"It's a mocha. And I know you said you don't like coffee, but it's good. I promise. Just try it."

He picked up the wide mug and brought it to his mouth. His lips pursed as he blew on the steaming liquid.

Madison's gaze focused on those lips and she held back a groan. *Just think, soon those lips could be all over my body.*

He took a sip and then swallowed. His expression remained the same. Then he raised his gaze to her questioning stare and gave a brief smile.

"Um, I like what you did with the fresh chocolate on top."

"Thanks. I'm a chocolate activist."

Time to get him thinking about something besides coffee. Madison walked back toward the counter, making sure her elbow nudged the straws so they tumbled onto the floor.

"Oops, I swear I am so clumsy sometimes." She bent over slowly and smiled as she felt her jeans pull downward with the motion. If she was correct—and from the sudden coolness on her bare skin she knew she was—her thong would be quite visible right now.

She picked up the straws, trying to figure out if his silence meant he was checking her out. She glanced over her shoulder to where he was sitting. Bingo. His eyes were focused very intently on her ass. They immediately shifted when he realized she had turned to look at him.

"It's good, huh?" she asked and turned her attention back to the straws. "Your mocha."

"It's...pretty damn good."

Madison clutched the straws in her hand and deposited them in the garbage.

She came back and sat beside him. He glanced everywhere but at her. His mocha, the door, the wall full of ceramic mugs.

"Gabe?"

His gaze turned to her, almost with reluctance.

"Can I get you anything else? Are you hungry? Do you want some biscotti? Maybe a bagel?" She ran her tongue over her bottom lip. "Or how about a blowjob?"

Chapter Two

Gabe bit back a groan. Thank God his lower body was hidden under the table, so that Madison couldn't see the way his cock jumped to immediate attention.

"I don't drink," he answered.

Her laugh turned husky. "I don't sell alcohol."

He knew he shouldn't have come today. He had every intention of *not* coming this weekend. But then he'd had a reason to come and he'd searched his house like an idiot trying to find that business card she'd handed him. For the life of him, he couldn't remember that reason now.

And, God, was he going to pay for it. *Just leave. Say no, and leave.* Or he could just pretend she hadn't said that last bit.

"Bagel."

She looked surprised, almost offended. "A...bagel?"

Maddie narrowed her eyes and leaned forward. "Okay, in case you haven't noticed, I'm not being subtle here, Gabe. What's the problem?"

Damn, she was aggressive. The blatant invitation made him grow harder. His hands itched to pull her onto his lap and rip the *They're Real* shirt off her full breasts and feel for himself. But that wasn't going to happen. He'd tempted fate enough by coming here, and damn it, he had to get out while he still could.

"I appreciate your directness, Maddie." He tried an apologetic smile, but his words were obviously not what she wanted to hear. "And I'd hoped to save you some embarrassment by not answering your question."

"So you won't consider having sex with me?" she demanded, standing and walking toward the door.

"That's not it," he answered in a tight voice, watching as her breasts jiggled with each movement. "A man would have to be an idiot to not want to have sex with you."

"All right, and we both know you're not an idiot. So, what's the problem?" She reached the door and flipped off the light switch, making the room dark except for the neon glow from the grocery store sign across the street.

Ah, shit, what was she up to now? He sighed, trying to keep his frustration at bay. "Look, Maddie, of course I want to have sex with you. You're a desirable woman. But I'm not going to do it. It's just not worth the trouble it'll create."

"That's so sweet. You sure know how to charm a woman. Good thing I'm a guarantee." She gave him a brief smile. "Is this about my brother?"

He hesitated. "Maddie, listen—"

"Let me save us both some time here." She crossed her arms over her stomach, grabbed the edge of her shirt, and pulled it over her head.

His mind went blank as he stared at her pale breasts covered by pink satin. Her nipples were already hard and distended against the fabric. Christ, she was beautiful.

Think about your old gym teacher, he told himself. *Don't let this happen.*

"Why do you want to sleep with me, Maddie?" he asked, his

26

voice rough, his mind trying to get control of his body. "Why me?"

"You're hot, Gabe." She walked over and pushed the table away from his chair, then swung a leg over his lap so that she straddled him. "And this bad boy here that I'm sitting on tells me how much you want me too."

His vision blurred as she moved herself against his erection. Even as he told himself to push her off him, his hips jerked upwards, grinding against her denim-clad heat.

His hands settled around her waist. "You know I don't do relationships, Maddie."

"Yes, I know. That's why you're perfect," she murmured and grabbed his hand, sliding it up her bare stomach to cover the curve of her breast. Her nipple pushed into the palm of his hand. "You're my rebound."

"Rebound?" His hand massaged the soft fullness of her breast under the satin. She arched into him, a silent request for more. His hand continued a light squeeze, his fingers sliding with slow deliberation toward her areola, and then out again.

"Bradley broke up with me." She groaned in frustration. "We're doing way too much talking here. Please..."

She'd had a boyfriend. And not too long ago. The thought sent some type of unfamiliar emotion through him. It wasn't exactly a good feeling, though.

She tried to move his hand to cover her nipple, but he wasn't ready to do it just yet.

If she were still nursing a broken heart, she would probably regret this later. He couldn't sleep with her. If she had been anybody else...anyone but Madison Phillips.

Even as the thought crossed his mind, his fingers moved to the center of her breast. Surrounding the firm nipple, rolling it and plucking it to further arousal.

"Gabe..." She gasped, grinding herself harder onto him. Her heat had grown more intense now, he could feel it. Smell it. He knew it by the slight glazing of her eyes.

The breath rushed from his lips. *Either stop this or finish it, Gabe.* Or maybe there was a way to do both.

He lifted Maddie off him and turned her around. With her now facing away from him, he pulled her back onto his lap. Her hands clutched his thighs as her head fell back against his chest.

"Gabe..."

"Trust me, Maddie," he whispered in her ear. Both of his hands came around to stroke her breasts through the bra, back and forth over her nipples until her breathing grew slow and labored.

He kept one hand on her nipple, bringing it to its full length, while his other hand moved down her belly to the button on her jeans. With familiar ease, he slipped the button through the hole and, with slow deliberation, unzipped her pants.

She wore a tiny, silky pink thong. He slipped a hand under the material and groaned. Obviously she liked to shave. Or wax. His cock jerked against her ass as he moved his fingers over her smooth mound. He cupped her for a moment before moving further down to tease the swollen lips of her sex.

She whimpered, her legs falling open and over his knees, as she leaned back against him. Her breast arched further into his hand, and he squeezed her nipple in a light pinch. He busied his other hand, parting her folds, circling the perimeter of her vagina. Then, when she sighed, he pushed a finger into her sheath. He hadn't found moisture until he'd slipped inside, and damn was she wet. She gave a guttural groan as her body clenched around him.

"Easy," he whispered, telling himself as much as her. He couldn't remember the last time a woman had gotten him this hot. The smell of her, the feel of her. She intoxicated him like a drug.

He withdrew his finger just a bit, and then plunged it back in. Her body seemed more relaxed this time. His thumb slipped up to stroke her clitoris, and he was again rewarded when she cried out.

"Oh, God, Gabe...don't stop. Don't stop doing that." She gasped as he again flicked his thumb over her.

He had no intention of stopping. He pulled his finger out from her hot channel, and then pushed back inside, this time adding a second finger. He closed his eyes, imagining it wasn't his fingers, but his cock inside her. He wanted release just as much as she did. But he wouldn't be having it.

His finger flicked faster over her, and she rotated against his hand. Her breath came quicker.

Her body started to tense, and he plunged his fingers to the hilt, letting his thumb drive her over the edge.

She contracted around him, gasping and shaking...and then collapsing back against him.

"Wow." Her breathless voice sounded almost too loud in the silence of the room. "Gabe. Wow."

She pulled away from him, stood, and turned around. "All right, your turn. Why don't you take off your shirt and I'll get to work on this guy."

Her cheeks were flushed from her orgasm, her blue eyes shining as she reached for the zipper on his jeans.

He caught her hand and gave it a gentle push away. "Enough, Maddie."

"Enough? We haven't even started." She laughed and put a hand over her breast, rolling her eyes toward the ceiling. "That was amazing. I can't wait to see what you've got going on down there."

"It's not going to happen."

She glanced back at him, seeming to at last hear him. "Excuse me? But you're still... You don't want to finish? Then what was all that? What just happened?"

"That was for you, Maddie. It's pretty damn obvious that I want you—"

"Don't swear at me," she interrupted, her eyes gleaming from anger now rather than sexual release. "You did that for me? For me?"

"I told you I wouldn't sleep with you—"

"I didn't ask you here to have you get me off, Gabe." She stepped away from him and zipped up her pants, found her top and then jerked it over her head.

"I have a vibrator. I asked you here to have sex. Full-blown penetration and all. If you couldn't bring yourself to do it, you should've told me to put my shirt back on and walked away."

He should have, but she'd made it damn difficult. Gabe shook his head. God, this had become a mess. She was right to be pissed.

"Listen, Maddie—"

"Get out of my shop."

"Maddie—"

"Get. Out." She wasn't yelling, but he'd have preferred it if she had been.

When she walked to the door and unlocked it, holding it open for him to leave, he knew this wasn't the best time to make amends.

"I'm sorry, Maddie." He walked toward her and laid a gentle hand on her shoulder. She shrugged it off and looked away, an obvious dismissal.

"And the name is Madison."

Gabe sighed and walked out the door.

Madison locked the door behind him and fought the urge to slide to the floor and scream with humiliation.

Of all the unbelievable ways to get rejected. What the hell had just happened? Had Gabe just given her a pity orgasm? No, that couldn't be it. It had been obvious that Gabe had wanted to finish the deed. But he hadn't. Why? It couldn't be because she was Eric's little sister. That would be ridiculous. Wouldn't it?

Of course it is, you twit. It was so stereotypical. So freaking cliché. And, unfortunately...so true. Gabe would not touch her because of who she was.

Her anger diminished somewhat. Maybe he hadn't handled the situation as well as she'd hoped, but in a way he was trying to be the good guy. He hadn't even kissed her, she realized and frowned. Was that a bad thing or a good thing? Would she have wanted the kissing?

Madison walked over to the table where Gabe's half-drunk mocha sat. As she picked it up, she had immediate flashbacks of what had happened ten minutes ago, and even though she'd just had the mother lode of all orgasms, she grew aroused again.

This was just wrong. There had to be a way around this, a way to make him realize how good the sex could be between them. He shouldn't have left with a hard-on, and she shouldn't have let him leave without experiencing that hard-on for herself.

She glanced down at the mocha and then took a tentative

sip. She winced and swallowed the lukewarm liquid. Gabe was also an extraordinary liar. The mocha tasted like crap. She'd burned the shot again. That still seemed to be the one thing she couldn't seem to get right.

She dumped the beverage down the sink and then proceeded to wash the mug, thinking about a couple of things. One, she would not be making drinks for customers any time soon. And, two, she had an orgasm to repay.

"It's a nonfat, tall, and, a, umm, double—wait, decaf latté. To go." Madison called out to Sarah as she shoved the customer's payment into the till.

Sarah laughed as she went to work creating the drink. "Just remember the system. Once you learn the system it'll get easier."

Madison shook her head, relieved that their morning rush seemed to be dying down. It was Wednesday. They'd had three somewhat successful days. She'd calculated a minimum of three hundred drinks needing to be sold a day to keep the shop up and running. So far they were averaging about two hundred. But the espresso was good—when Sarah made it—and word of mouth seemed to be spreading fast.

She'd also allowed enough money in the bank and on her credit card to ensure that they had some leeway for a year or so.

Sarah handed the customer his drink, and after he left the shop, they were once again alone.

"Are you going to kill me?" Madison asked Sarah with a wince. "I know this has got to be way more chaotic than you expected."

"This is fine, Madison, don't worry about it." Sarah went to the sink to wash her hands. "Trust me, I've seen and done much worse."

"I promise I'll hire someone else on soon." Madison knew she would've been toast if she didn't have Sarah. The perky, curly-haired blonde had saved her butt. "Take a break, Sarah. Lord knows you've earned it."

"Thanks." Sarah tossed the towel she'd dried her hands on back onto the counter. "I'm going to run over to the grocery store deli and grab something to eat."

"You can help yourself to any of the baked goods we sell, if you want," Madison offered.

"I would." Sarah grinned. "But if it's not deep-fried, I'm not craving it. And now that you know my vice, I'll be back in a few."

Madison laughed and watched her leave the shop. How did the girl keep in such good shape and eat such crap? She had to be one of those women who ran three miles every morning.

She helped herself to a bagel and pulled out one of the packets of cream cheese. She'd just finished slicing the bagel when the door chimed.

A thought hit her. She would have to make the drinks. Damn, what a way to lose a new customer.

"Hello," she called out and then glanced up. "What can I— oh. It's just you." Her tone lost all trace of friendliness as the chaotic emotions from Sunday resurfaced.

Obviously Gabe was working, because he was dressed in his police uniform. Gun, badge, tight pants and all. And, Lord, if he didn't look good in it.

"Don't you have some bad guys to chase or something?" she queried with false innocence. "Or if this is your break, shouldn't you be at the local donut shop?"

"Out to draw blood this morning, aren't we, Maddie?"

And he still insisted on calling her Maddie. She forced a smile. She might be trying to get him into bed, but that didn't mean she had to forgive him for Sunday night.

"Can I get you anything, Gabe?"

His eyes darkened, and she realized she'd said the same thing to him on Sunday. And look what that had led to.

"I want to apologize," he admitted after a moment. "Again."

"All right." She gave a slight nod and then her smile widened. "Let me make you a mocha."

She saw the flicker of panic in his eyes and reveled in it as she started to prepare the shot for his drink.

"I thought you had some other girl working with you," he asked, an obvious attempt to sound casual. "Someone else who was making the drinks?"

"Oh, yeah." She gestured out the door. "She's on her lunch and just ran to get food. But you seemed to like mine on Sunday, should there be a problem with today?"

She'd meant her statement to have a double meaning, and he must have noticed it because he didn't answer. Instead his eyes dropped to her breasts, which were covered by a white shirt and black apron.

"Well, I sure as hell liked your outfit better on Sunday." His voice had dropped an octave as he took a step closer to the counter.

She raised an eyebrow as she added chocolate syrup and then the grated chocolate to the drink. "I'm impressed. I thought I might have scared you off after what happened."

"You kicked me out."

"You deserved it." She handed him the mocha. "I made it to

go. I'm sure you have a route to be patrolling or something."

He took the mocha, glancing at it with a tight smile, and then reached for his wallet. "How much do I owe you?"

"It's on the house."

"Maddie—Madison," he corrected himself. "I just wanted to make sure there weren't any bad feelings about Sunday. I mean, I don't want this to affect my relationship with you and your family."

"Oh, it won't." She put on her most saccharine smile. "I have no problem with having you—my brother's best friend— give me an orgasm. Even if you seem to. And I have no plans to tell my family about it either. So, look at that, we're fine."

He seemed skeptical by her response. "So all is forgiven and forgotten?"

"Yes and no. Yes, you're forgiven." Madison stepped out from behind the counter and took the few remaining steps that separated them. She whispered against his ear, "And, no, nothing's forgotten."

Her hand crept down his body and squeezed with just enough pressure between his legs.

"Maddie." He groaned.

"I see, or feel, that I missed out on quite a bit Sunday." She stepped back and smiled. "You are nowhere near being forgotten. We have a lot to do before I file you away as a memory."

"You have got to be the most forward woman I've ever met." He laughed, this time with real amusement. "And I've met some. How late are you open?"

Madison walked back behind the counter, making sure her hips swayed in a provocative manner. "Six. You'd better head out now, Officer Martinez."

"Hold up—I didn't come just to apologize, Maddie." He shook his head, as if to clear it. "On Sunday I forgot to warn you about a robber who's been hitting local espresso stands and shops—"

"Oh, yeah, the Coffee Robber or something?" She shrugged. "Yeah, Sarah said something about him. I'm not worried."

"The Espresso Bandit. I'm just asking you to be vigilant, Maddie," he warned and started walking backwards toward the door, his gaze never leaving hers. "You're not going to close alone tonight, are you?"

"I think Sarah is staying. But we'll see how it goes." She waved her hand toward him. "Anyway, go on now, Gabe. God knows you should have some real emergency by now to respond to."

"This isn't over, Maddie."

She smiled, her eyes offering another invitation. "You're right. It isn't."

"I meant this discussion about what's going on with us." He reached the door and his hand paused on the handle. "If I can, I'll drop in later tonight when you close. We need more time to talk."

"I was hoping you'd say that." She grabbed her purse and pulled a key out. "I had a spare made for you. Let yourself in since I'll probably be in the back counting down the tills."

She set the key in his hand and folded his fingers around it. "See you tonight."

"I said if I can. I'm not promising—"

"I'll see you tonight." Her smile widened.

Sarah pulled open the door at that moment, carrying her lunch from the grocery store deli. She glanced at Gabe's mocha, and then to Madison in surprise.

Madison grinned and waved goodbye to Gabe. "Enjoy your mocha."

Gabe sighed and walked out the door.

After he left, Sarah carried her food behind the counter and sat on the stool.

"He was pretty cute. But I'm surprised you'd risk serving a cop one of your mochas." Sarah grinned as she pulled out a plastic bag full of greasy-smelling potato wedges. "How did it come out?"

"I'm sure it tastes awful," Madison admitted, watching as his squad car pulled out of the parking lot. "But trust me, he deserved it. I know him."

"Ah." Sarah gave her a sideways glance and teased, "Know him as in the biblical sense?"

Madison snapped her focus back to Sarah. "Not yet, but ask me again in a few days."

Gabe took a drink of his lemonade, cringing as the Mariners gave up another run to the Yankees.

"Ouch, this is hard to watch." Eric stood and walked into Gabe's kitchen. "Do you have anything to drink besides lemonade?"

"There's Coke in the fridge or bottled water."

Eric had shown up at his apartment wanting to watch the game and catch up. And although Gabe had planned to go see Madison tonight, it would have to wait. Besides, he was pretty close to reaching this week's quota for temptation.

Eric reappeared with a Coke in his hand. "Lannie and I set a date. It's going to be the last Saturday in August."

"I'll mark it on my calendar." The televised game broke for a commercial, and his thoughts went back to Maddie. He wondered if he should be feeling guiltier, especially with Eric sitting right next to him.

As if he somehow knew Gabe was thinking about his sister, Eric brought her up.

"So I checked out Madison's shop today. Not bad," he stated. "I'm pretty proud of my little sister, opening her own business and all. I think she saw Mom do it and wanted to try her hand at it."

"Right," Gabe replied, thinking about the upscale fashion boutique Lillian Phillips owned. "Why coffee though?"

"I believe she said she fell in love with the charm of cappuccinos in Italy or something." Eric shrugged. "I'm not sure. She sure does drink enough of the stuff."

That didn't mean she knew how to make one. Gabe winced as he recalled the mocha from Sunday and the one this afternoon. Today's mocha had gotten dumped into the trash bin just outside her shop. He'd been discreet enough so that she hadn't noticed—well, he hoped she hadn't noticed.

"I worry about her, though," Eric admitted. "I've been watching the news a lot. The past month there's been a series of robberies at coffee places. I think they're calling him the Espresso Bandit. Have you heard of him?"

Gabe turned his gaze away from the game that had come back on. "He was the first thing we discussed during briefing this morning. Why?"

"Well, I just heard one of his victims died this afternoon. It was all over the news."

Tension coiled through Gabe's neck and spread down his body. He'd known the Bandit had shot someone in a robbery last week, but last he'd heard, the victim was still in critical condition.

"Does your sister watch the news?"

"Does Madison watch the news?" Eric laughed, as if it were a hilarious question. "Try *Desperate Housewives* and *Oprah.*"

Gabe stood, a sudden premonition tingling at the back of his neck. He pulled her business card from his wallet and grabbed the phone, punching in the digits.

After seven rings, she still hadn't answered. He hung up and glanced at the clock. Five after six. It was possible that she'd pre-closed the store and had gotten out right at six. Definitely possible, but it didn't seem too likely.

Eric gave him a hard look. "We should go down there and make sure she's okay."

"I'll grab my keys."

Gabe told himself he was overreacting as they made the drive over. He'd discussed the Espresso Bandit with her this afternoon. Of course she would be taking precautions.

Chapter Three

"No, no," Madison waved her hand at Sarah. "Go ahead and go home. Don't even worry about it. Shoot, you've already worked a twelve-hour day."

"Well, since I'm going to school to be a nurse, I might as well get used to it." Sarah laughed as she pulled her jacket on and then hesitated. "Are you sure, Madison? I feel kinda bad leaving you here all alone."

"I've just got a few things left to do," Madison promised. "I'll be outta here in ten minutes. Go. Turn off the lights on your way out."

"All right, I'll see you tomorrow. Don't forget to lock the door behind me."

Madison watched her go and then smiled. Good. She would be all by herself when Gabe dropped by. She wouldn't fail in seducing him tonight. She refused to.

But first things first. She went to the front door and locked it, giving it a tug to make sure she'd secured it. Then she emptied both of the garbage cans up front and carried the two bags to the back door. She slipped outside and then hesitated. It sure was creepy back here. During the day it wasn't so bad, but at night...

Don't be so paranoid. You'll be back in less than a minute. She hurried around to the side of building where the

Dumpsters were.

It was already getting dark, and the shadows had her heart pounding. She hurled the bags over the edge of the Dumpster and then sprinted back to her shop.

Madison slipped inside the back room and froze, hearing a sound come from the front of the shop. There was someone inside. She started to turn and run out the back door again, then stopped. *You idiot, it's only Gabe.*

Although he might've shown some manners and announced his presence, saving her from getting the snot scared out of her.

Well, revenge could be sweet. Madison grinned as she began to strip off all her clothes. When she got down to her bikini panties and matching bra, she crept into the front room. *Let him say no to this.*

She hesitated a second, that rational voice in her head bringing up the *Madison, what if it isn't Gabe?* factor. She shrugged it off as she spotted him facing away from her near the cash register.

Tiptoeing right up behind him she grabbed his ass and whispered in his ear, "Hey there, sexy."

She realized right away that it wasn't Gabe by the butt. She'd given Gabe's a thorough inspection, and this one was way too soft and fleshy. If that wasn't enough, the man turned around and glared at her with furious blue eyes.

Oh, God. She should have listened to the voice in her head. Madison screamed and executed a quick twist in an attempt to get to the back door.

He caught her and slammed her against the counter.

"Where in the hell did you come from?" he demanded in disbelief, not seeming to expect a response. His eyes dropped and she groaned as he looked her up and down. "Were you expecting me, darling?"

Her face crinkled in disgust. God, why had she thought that it would be a good idea to run out here like an attendee at a streaking party?

"This is my store," she replied, trying to keep her voice calm and authoritative. "And I'd suggest you get out before I call the police."

The gun he pressed against her temple had her blinking in disbelief. Gun? He was going to threaten her with a freaking gun?

"In case you haven't figured it out, darling," he muttered. "I'm robbing you."

Robbery? In her first week in business? Her anger level shot up a notch.

Damn. This must be the guy who Gabe had warned her about. *This can't be happening.* Fury spread throughout her body. *Not to me.* She pushed the gun off her temple and glared at him.

"Oh, no you're not. Pick another business, asshole." Had she just said that?

She had. And the gun that slapped across her face, sending her sprawling to the floor, seemed a good reminder.

Tears sprang to her eyes from the fierce pain. It caused a throbbing heat to spread from her jaw all the way down her neck.

Madison's original burst of adrenaline died. God, that had been a stupid thing to do. Panic and fear clawed at her belly.

"Okay," she whispered. "What do you want?"

"Get up." He grabbed her by the elbow, jerking her to her feet. "Open the register."

"There's nothing in it." Her fingers fumbled with the key. The register sprang open and displayed an empty drawer. "All the money is in the safe and the deposit bag is in the back."

He jerked her away from the register and toward the back room.

Madison's blood pounded so hard from fear, she was sure he could hear it. When they reached the back, he forced her onto her knees beside the safe and she went to work opening it. Her fingers trembled as she spun the dial.

The safe swung open and the man started grabbing fistfuls of cash, stuffing them into his bag. Then he dumped the till money, all ready for the next day, in as well.

It's just money, she told herself. *He'll be gone in a minute, and then it'll just be missing money.*

She glanced up at him to see what the holdup was. *The holdup.* She almost let out a hysterical giggle at her own silent joke. He stared down at her with those same cold blue eyes.

"Turn around and lie down on your stomach."

She blinked at him, a new terror seizing her. "Why—"

"Just do it!"

She turned around and slid forward on her stomach. The tiled floor rubbed like ice against her naked skin and she started to shiver. Oh God. He was going to tie her up. Or rape her. Or...kill her. She heard him take the safety off.

"Sorry, honey. Wrong place, wrong time."

Madison went numb and closed her eyes, beginning to pray.

"Madison!"

Is this what almost dying does to you? Makes you hear voices?

"Son of a bitch!"

She opened her eyes as the man behind her cursed. He grabbed her purse off the desk and bolted out the back door.

The next second Gabe came running into the back room, a gun in his hand.

"Gabe?" She pulled herself off the ground. "He ran out the back door!"

Gabe's gaze ripped from her near-naked body as he tore after him. A second later Eric came through the front door and into the back room.

"Madison." He whipped off his jacket and flung it around her. "Here, sit down while I call the police."

She slipped on his jacket and edged her shaking body into the chair at her desk, laying her head on her hands. Oh God. Oh God. He'd been about to shoot her. She knew it.

When Gabe returned a moment later, she looked up, hoping he'd be dragging the robber behind him. He gave a grim shake of his head.

That meant he was still out there. The man who had been about to kill her two minutes ago remained free.

Madison stood, her legs unsteady.

"I'll be right back." She pushed Gabe out of the way and locked herself into the tiny bathroom. She had the urge to vomit but couldn't seem to make it happen. Instead she turned on the water and began rinsing her face.

Gabe waited outside the door, relieved to see her come out a few minutes later. He did a quick check, trying to figure out if she might lose it or get hysterical. She appeared calm and collected, though. Funny, he wouldn't have expected that from her.

She glanced around. "Where did Eric go?"

"He's out talking to the police. They'll be back to interview you any minute." He pushed a hand through his hair. "How did he get in? Did you lock the door?"

"Yes!" She shook her head. "I have no idea."

There was no sign of forced entry. Gabe glanced over at the bathroom she'd just come out of, an uneasy feeling in his gut. It was entirely possible the robber had gone the *wait in the bathroom until he's alone* route.

He turned back to Maddie and really looked at her, not just the passing, agitated glance. His gaze drifted to her bruised cheek and he clenched his fists. The blood pounded in his veins and his vision blurred. Somehow he managed to keep his voice neutral when he asked, "He pistol-whipped you?"

"Is that what it's called? I always wondered what that term meant." Madison smiled and then winced in pain. "Yeah, I guess he did."

Unwillingly, his gaze took in her luscious curves underneath Eric's wool jacket again. Christ, she was sexy.

How much of an asshole are you, Gabe? Thinking about getting her flat on her back right after she's had a gun to her head?

He cleared his throat. "Did he make you take off your clothes? Did he—"

"Umm, no." Her face went red and she glanced down at her bare feet. "I did that on my own."

"What?" He blinked. "Why?"

Two officers came around back and called out a greeting.

Madison leaned forward and hissed, "Because I thought he was you. This doesn't make it into the report."

His dick hardened at her words, and he cursed. This wasn't exactly the time or place to be springing wood.

"Miss Phillips?" One of the officers, a female, approached her.

"Yes." She nodded.

"We're going to ask you some questions about what happened..."

Gabe let the officer do her job, but wished to hell he could be the one questioning Madison. Since he was off duty he was denied that right, but at least he could be by her side while it happened. His attention snapped back to the question they were asking her.

"The Espresso Bandit has been very consistent in what he wears when he strikes. I assume he was wearing a black ski mask, black shirt and black pants?"

"Yes, to the black pants and black shirt. And no to the ski mask."

"He wasn't wearing a mask?" Gabe repeated in disbelief, and snapped his mouth shut when the officer gave him a sharp glance.

"He didn't realize I was here," she explained. She licked her lips and cast a warning glance at Gabe. "You see, I was changing in the back when he came in through the front. He must have assumed I was gone. I heard a noise and went to investigate."

The officer nodded. "And that would explain your state of dress?"

Madison nodded.

"Miss Phillips," the officer gentled her tone. "I need to know if there was any kind of assault—"

"No. The whole thing happened in like ten minutes." She closed her eyes. "He was going to kill me if Gabe and Eric hadn't shown up."

"You're the first person he's held up who is capable of identifying him, which is even more vital now that one of his victims has died."

The fury at how close to death she'd been washed over Gabe in waves. God. Why hadn't she listened to him?

"You'll need to come down to the station first thing in the morning. We'll need you to work with our sketch artist so we can get his picture out," the officer stated and went on with more questions.

Gabe walked to the front of the shop, where Eric paced in obvious distress. He hadn't thought anyone could be more furious than he was right now, but Eric seemed to be giving him some competition.

"She's all right, isn't she?" Eric asked, looking up at him with cold eyes. "I mean, she can identify him. What if he comes back?"

"I'm sure we'll have an officer guarding the shop," Gabe assured him, although something else still worried him. "She told the officer the robber took her purse."

"Damn. She'll have to cancel all her credit cards and let the bank know. I wonder if she had any cash." Eric didn't seem to understand his point, but suddenly stiffened. "He knows where she lives."

"He was going to kill her." Gabe forced his voice to sound calm. "We got here right as the son of a bitch had his gun to her head. It seems he didn't like the idea of someone being able to identify him."

"She can't go home." Eric shook his head. "He's going to be waiting for her."

My thoughts exactly. Gabe's voice turned firm. "Take her to your parents'. She needs to have someone with her all the time."

"My parents are in their mid-sixties. What are they going to protect her with? Social Security?"

"You and Lannie—"

"I can't bring Lannie into this, Gabe. I won't risk the lives of two women I love. Please," Eric insisted. "You know I would never ask this of you, but, my God, this is Maddie. You are the one and only person I'd trust with her life."

Gabe agreed with him one hundred percent. His initial reaction was to drag her off and lock her up in his house. He knew he was damn capable of protecting Maddie, and would kill anyone who tried to hurt her. But then he realized the position he'd be putting them in.

Eric didn't know their recent history. Gabe closed his eyes, and had an immediate flashback to her hot body riding his fingers. She would be safe with him in some ways, but not others.

"Gabe, there's things you don't know. Things we don't like to talk about." Eric scratched the back of his neck and looked down. "Something bad happened to Madison a long time ago. She was too young to even remember. But there are reasons why we tend to worry."

Something bad had happened to Maddie? Gabe's gut clenched. How bad?

Eric shook his head. "Look, the bottom line is I really need you to protect her."

He wanted her safe. And he knew he could protect her. But still he hesitated. "I'm not sure I'm the best person for her."

"And I'm sure you are, Gabe. Please say yes."

"Say yes to what?" Madison asked as she came out of the back room, the two officers following her. The cops nodded at them on their way out of the shop.

"I think you should stay with Gabe for a while," Eric informed her. "Until they catch the Espresso Bandit."

Her eyes took on a speculative look. "Why would I do that?"

"He knows where you live." Gabe met her gaze as he dropped the ominous news. "You're the one person who's seen his face and knows what he looks like. I don't think he took your purse for monetary reasons."

Madison nodded, even as she felt the color drain from her face. She didn't doubt for a minute that this Espresso Bandit would be caught, but until that happened, she wasn't about to be a sitting duck for him. She felt safe with Gabe, he would never let anything happen to her. And staying with him wouldn't be such a hardship. She tried to replace the horrible images of the robbery with more stimulating ones of Gabe. It helped a little to ease her inner turmoil.

"Fine. I'll stay with Gabe." She glanced up at him.

Her thoughts must have been reflected in her eyes because he met her gaze and she knew he was silently rebuking all her plans at seduction. There was a long matching of wills before he turned to face Eric.

"Bring her car back to your parents' and I'll take her to her apartment to pack up some things."

Eric gave her a long hug and the quick *you'll be all right* bit, and then walked out the door.

Madison watched as Gabe locked up the front door and turned off the lights. He looked so tall and strong. So invincible. She didn't doubt for a minute he would keep her safe.

She cleared her throat. "I'll go put some clothes on before we leave."

Gabe glanced back at her, his expression strained. "Please

do."

When they reached her apartment, he took the keys from Madison's hand and unlocked the door, gesturing for her to keep silent and wait while he stepped inside. He doubted that the robber would be so brazen as to show up right away, but he wasn't taking any chances.

While she waited in the entryway, he walked around her apartment, his expression growing grimmer by the minute.

"Okay, if you think I'm going to just sit here—" Madison announced, coming up behind him. "What's wrong? You look upset."

"He was here."

"Oh, no..." She looked around her apartment and frowned at him. "How can you tell?"

Gabe turned to her in disbelief. It couldn't be possible. It could not be possible that someone would choose to live like this.

"It looks like a tornado touched down in your bedroom," he stated. "Are you telling me that this was your doing?"

Madison's eyes flashed as she folded her arms across her chest. "I was looking for my black pants."

"Well, I hope you found them," he drawled. "I need to use your restroom. Pack a bag and we'll get out of here."

"Fine." She hesitated. "I have some bras and panties hanging in the bathroom—just push them aside or ignore them."

Gabe gave an inward groan. *God, does that mean the bathroom is as much of a disaster as the rest of her house?*

It was, he realized a moment later, as he waded through pieces of hanging black lace.

If she'd clean up the apartment a little, one could almost see how much the place must be worth. It was a spacious apartment with a view of the Seattle waterfront.

He glanced back at the bra, his lips curving. Even while telling himself not to do it, he leaned forward to check the tag on the bra.

Victoria's Secret. Nice. 34D. Very nice. His fingers glided over the lace before he let the bra fall back against the door. Great, more fuel for his forbidden fantasies.

This would be hell, having her stay with him. To be sleeping a room away from her. He'd already been praying that his self-restraint would be on par with Maddie's bad intentions.

Eric had been right about one thing, though. She would be safe with him. And until the Espresso Bandit was caught, he didn't want anyone to have to worry about her safety.

Gabe dried his hands on a pink towel and glanced in the mirror. For a minute he fantasized about the idea of him being the one to arrest the Espresso Bandit. Get him alone and show the asshole what it felt like to get the shit kicked out of him.

He finished in the bathroom and went to sit on the plush couch in Maddie's living room. She still appeared to be packing. He could hear her singing an off-key rendition of a Madonna song. He winced. Very off-key. Good thing she hadn't attempted a career in music.

"I'm almost done, Gabe," she called from her room. "Feel free to help yourself to anything in the fridge. I think I have some leftover Pad Thai with tofu."

"Thanks, but you lost me at tofu."

She emerged from the bedroom carrying a suitcase three times the size she should've needed.

He plucked it from her grasp, aware that she was

struggling. "You ready?"

"Almost," she answered, pulling a rubber band off her wrist and fixing her hair into a ponytail. The band snapped off her fingers and flew across the room.

"Damn." She hurried over to where it landed, bending over to retrieve it.

For the briefest moment she gave him the most tantalizing view of her tight ass. He stifled a groan, wanting to pull down her jeans and panties and fuck her from behind.

She straightened and finished pulling her hair back. "I'm hungry. Can we go grab dinner somewhere?"

Gabe went from having kinky thoughts to getting seriously annoyed. Where did her budget end? Did she eat every meal out?

"I've got food at my house." He ushered her out the door and locked it behind them. "I'll cook you something."

She gave him a dubious look. "You cook?"

"It comes out edible. So try not to complain too much while I'm stuck babysitting you," he replied, further annoyed by her skepticism.

Her eyes widened and he saw a flash of hurt in them. Shit. That had been below the belt. This situation hadn't been her choice.

They took the elevator downstairs and walked out to his vintage Chevelle. He unlocked the trunk and heard the tiny gasp that came from Maddie. Her face was pale when he glanced at her; her head turned at an awkward angle, like she was trying not to look in the trunk.

"What's wrong?"

"Nothing." Her tone grew tight. "It's just...nothing."

He slammed the trunk, watching as the tension in her body

visibly eased. Hmm. That was odd. He thought about pressing the issue, but decided against it.

"I'm sorry, Maddie. About what I said upstairs. I didn't mean it," he said instead, gentling his tone and holding the passenger door open for her.

She blinked at him, looking stunned. Then she shook her head as she climbed into the seat and shut the door.

Why did she look so shocked? Gabe gave her another glance and climbed into the driver's side of the car. He almost asked what he'd said, and then stopped himself. Some things were better left alone.

Chapter Four

Madison sat in the passenger seat and stared out the window in amazement. She couldn't recall if a man had ever apologized to her before. Maybe her brother and father. But a man she'd been interested in who would apologize and admit he was wrong? The whole concept seemed a bit mind boggling. *Or maybe I've just dated losers.*

Her thoughts turned back to that other awkward moment. When he'd opened the trunk and she'd nearly fainted.

If there was one thing she didn't want Gabe to know about, it was that. Her irrational fear of car trunks. Just the thought of her reaction a moment ago sent a wave of humiliation through her. Who the hell was afraid of car trunks? She closed her eyes. But the phobia went back for as long as she could remember.

She'd owned two cars since the day she'd gotten her driver's license, and in neither vehicle had she ever opened the trunk. If her family and friends knew about her fear, they never commented on it.

"You doing okay?" He glanced over at her.

She nodded and took a deep, calming breath in. *Relax, Madison. Relax.*

The ride to Gabe's took about a half-hour. He lived in Edmonds, a suburb about fifteen miles north of Seattle. He stopped the car in front of a small house and she looked around in surprise. They were just a couple of blocks away from the ferry dock in a fairly nice neighborhood.

She hesitated and then asked, "Do you rent this house?"

He gave her a brief glance before climbing out of the car. She followed suit, meeting up with him at the back of the car. She didn't want him to think her a total freak. He unlocked the trunk and she kept her gaze carefully averted.

"My aunt lived here. She left me the house when she died."

Madison turned her gaze back to the house. It appeared small and quaint on the outside. She'd known that Gabe had left California to come live with his aunt at the age of thirteen. But she never knew the details as to why.

"You went to the same prep school as my brother...in Seattle." She didn't want to pry, but curiosity got the better of her. "Wouldn't it have been easier to attend school in a district nearer to you?"

Gabe grabbed her suitcase and his mouth curled into a fond smile.

"My aunt wanted me to get a good education. She managed to pay the outrageous tuition. To this day, I still don't know how she did it." He unlocked the door to his house and swung it inward.

"So you drove down to Seattle every day?" She followed him into the house. When he flipped on the light switch, she gave a sigh of appreciation. What a beautiful house. Hardwood floors, area rugs, oak furniture mixed with a plush couch and chair. She turned her delighted gaze toward him and found him staring at her.

"No. I took the bus every day at five a.m., with two transfers, to get to school. Just so I could have the same opportunities as the rich kids."

Her enthusiasm dimmed somewhat. It was apparent that—in case she hadn't realized it before—he was telling her just how different their worlds had been. How much she'd taken for granted.

"You were blessed. I never met your aunt, but she always sounded amazing." She had the urge to go over and hug him, kiss his cheek, but knew it wouldn't go over well.

"She was." Gabe turned and walked down the hall. "Come on, I'll show you where your room is."

Madison followed him down the short hallway. He stopped in front of a door across from what she assumed to be his room.

The room he led her into was minimal. A cream-colored quilt lay atop the twin bed under the window and an antique dresser sat in the corner, with a wicker chair next to it. Such a charming room.

He must have mistaken her silence for distaste because his tone grew harsh as he said, "I'm sure it's not up to your usual standards, but it should do."

"It's perfect, Gabe." She turned around to face him. "I'm a little confused. Did I run over your dog or something? Where is this hostility coming from? There've been a couple of barbed remarks tonight."

His glance dropped to her mouth, and his body tensed. *It's me. Being here.* He still fought the inevitable. He was so damned determined to be the good guy.

"Gabe." She took a step toward him, wanting to feel her mouth under his. She hadn't kissed him yet. He'd given her a mind-blowing orgasm, and she hadn't even kissed him. That needed to be remedied.

Her tongue slicked over her lips as she glanced up at him. His gaze caught the movement and she could have sworn he groaned, but he still kept the distance between them.

56

"I thought you were hungry, Maddie."

She ran her hands down his chest, her fingers clenching the material of his shirt.

"I am." She reached up to the back of his head and pulled his mouth down onto hers.

His lips were soft, yet firm as she moved her mouth against them. She ran her tongue over his bottom lip then gave it a gentle bite with her teeth.

He must have given up any idea of refusing, because his hands grasped her hips and jerked her firmly against his body as he backed her up against the wall.

He pulled the rubber band free from her hair and threaded his fingers through the strands that fell to her shoulders. He tilted her head a bit and deepened the kiss, his tongue thrusting into the cavern of her mouth.

Madison's head spun and she realized she had just lost control of the situation. Not that she cared. This was the exact response she'd been hoping to get from him.

His knee slid between her legs and rubbed against her throbbing sex through her jeans. He groaned again, and she answered with one of her own.

She stroked her tongue against his, loving the warm, abrasive textures rubbing together. His hand came up to cup the side of her face and she yelped in pain.

"Maddie...?" He pulled back, looking dazed.

"My jaw is just a little tender." *No!* Madison wanted to smack herself. She reached for him and tried to bring his mouth back down to her. "We can work around it."

"Shit." His hand gentled against her cheek as he stepped back from her. "I forgot that he hit you. Let's get some ice on that."

"No. No, no!" She grabbed his arm. "Let's not. Let's stay here and you can keep on kissing me until my knees go weak again—"

Gabe took her hand and pulled her into the kitchen after him. He urged her into a chair and went to the freezer, pulling out a bag of frozen vegetables.

Madison shook her head in disgust. She'd almost had him. Had been so close to having him. But no. She had to let a little bruise get in the way.

He handed her the vegetables wrapped in a paper towel and she obediently placed them against her cheek, wincing at the abrupt coldness.

"Now, let's get you something to eat." He cast her a sharp look as he opened the fridge. "And I mean food."

Madison sighed and gave him a wry smile. "You can't blame a girl for trying."

He laughed as he pulled a carton of eggs and a pack of tortillas out of the fridge.

"Do you like eggs?"

"Yeah, that's fine."

"All right." He turned on the stove and sat a frying pan on top of the burner. "I'm going to make you something my aunt used to make. It's called *tortilla con huevo.*"

"Hmm." She watched as he added a glob of butter to the pan, making a mental note to attend an extra spinning class this week.

Gabe tore a small hole in the middle of a corn tortilla, and laid it into the cast-iron skillet.

Curious, she stood and went to lean on the counter next to him, watching him prepare her food. When the tortilla had turned a light brown, he cracked an egg over the hole and allowed it to cook.

After a moment, he grabbed a spatula and flipped the tortilla so the yolk of the egg peeked through the gap.

"Wow." She glanced at him. "I'm impressed. That looks great. Fattening, but great."

"Oh, please." He shook his head and flipped the concoction out of the pan and onto a plate. "Do you want salsa?"

"Oh, yeah. Pile it on, baby." She accepted the steaming plate and a fork from him a minute later.

"You think you'll want another one?"

"No, this'll do me." She took a seat at the antique table in the dining room. "Aren't you going to eat?"

"Eric and I got something before we..."

Before they'd shown up at her shop. She knew the rest of what he hadn't said. Her stomach rolled with the memories and she almost lost her appetite. Squelching down any further reaction, she lifted a bite to her mouth.

The buttery tortilla combined with the rich moist egg yolk had her moaning her appreciation.

"You like?" Gabe's eyes darkened as he watched her mouth.

"I really, really like." She'd seen his reaction, but continued to eat. After she'd polished off most of it, she laid down her fork. "You know what else I like?"

He took a seat next to her. "I can guess."

She raised an eyebrow and leaned back in her chair. "I like to be on top. I like to ride a man like he's a mechanical bull."

Gabe forced a laugh as the image of her riding him floated through his head. "I guessed wrong."

His ran his gaze over her. She was so damn sexy with her

hair falling around her face and partially covering one of her eyes. Eyes that twinkled a challenge to him. She lifted a finger to her mouth and licked it clean of any trace of yolk.

"I like a lot of things, Gabe." Her voice grew breathy. "Aren't you at all curious to discover them?"

Hell, yes. Right now he wanted to be that bull. God, he wanted her. He wanted her on the table. On the couch. On the bathroom rug.

"Some things are better left unknown, Maddie." He kept his voice neutral.

"Why is it so taboo to sleep with your friend's sister?" she asked with genuine confusion. "I'm not unfamiliar with your sexual habits, Gabe. You're not the type to decline strings-free sex..."

He stood. "Maddie—"

"Unless you're not attracted to me." Doubt flickered through in her eyes, and she stood, moving to stand right in front of him. "I mean, I know men can fake it. And if that's the case then—"

"How could I not be attracted to you?" he snapped and grabbed her hand, pressing it against his hardening cock. "Do you feel what you do to me? Are you happy now? Is that what you wanted?"

"Yes, Gabe." Her gaze flicked up to meet his with fierce determination. "This is exactly what I want."

His fingers closed around her wrist and he pried her hand away, already regretting his decision to have a hands-on demonstration.

"You know where your room is, Maddie. Go to bed." He set her aside. "It's almost midnight and we've got a long day ahead of us tomorrow."

"Are you kidding me?" She threw her hands in the air. "And they call women teases? You're sending me to bed fully aroused, do you realize that?"

"What do you want me to do?" he demanded in frustration. "Like it or not, Maddie, there is a rule. An unspoken rule between friends, and I respect your brother too much to have sex with you."

"Don't think of me as Eric's sister." She groaned and pressed her body against his. She took his hand and mimicked his earlier motions, placing it between her legs.

Through the thin layer of her pants, he could feel her heat and the hint of dampness. He groaned, knowing he couldn't take her the way he wanted to. And if he gave her the orgasm she wanted, she'd hate him later. Then again, that might not be such a bad thing.

She made the decision for him and shoved his hand away from her. "Fine. I'll go to bed."

Disappointment stabbed through him, even when he knew it should be relief.

"But take this memory with you." She stepped forward and lowered her voice. "I am going to be lying in your spare bed touching myself. Think about me rubbing my hot, swollen, wet—"

"Madison!"

She gave his erection a pointed glance.

"Sleep well, Gabe," she murmured, and turned to go to her room. It was all he could do not to follow.

An hour later she lay in bed wide-awake with frustration. Despite her declaration to accomplish her own orgasm, she was far from it.

She traced her finger over the smooth folds between her legs, playing with the moisture she found and rubbing a finger over her clitoris. Imagining it was Gabe didn't help, because her soft finger couldn't compare to his thick, calloused ones.

Madison knew she had it bad when she couldn't even bring her own release. She wanted him so much that it became almost a physical pain.

She squeezed her eyes shut and rolled over onto her side, curling her legs up toward her chest and willing the ache between her legs to disappear.

It took almost another hour before she slipped into a light sleep, and instead of being comforted, she found herself reliving the robbery. Except this time, the robber pulled the trigger.

She jerked upright with a cry, dragging the sheets around her. A moment later her door burst open and Gabe's silhouette filled the doorway.

"Maddie?" He shut the door and came over to the bed. "What's wrong? I heard you cry out."

She turned her head away before he could see the shine of tears in her eyes. The dream had been too real.

"Did you dream about him?" Gabe asked, his voice soft. "It's all right, Maddie. It's normal. I haven't seen you break down once yet."

"I'm not the type to break down," she mumbled. She urged herself to regain control and not lose it. But the back of her throat burned from choking back the tears, and soon she stopped fighting.

The tears ran down her cheeks and she kept her face averted, trying to hide them.

"Maddie..." He pulled her unresisting body into his arms, sliding back against the bedpost to support them. She buried her head against his chest.

"It's just sexual tension combined with the post-traumatic stress." She tried to laugh and it came out choked. "Nothing to worry about. It'd all go away if you'd just have sex with me."

"You don't need to make it a joke, Maddie," he murmured. "It's nothing to be ashamed or embarrassed about."

Wasn't it? She hated that she was crying on Gabe's shoulder. He was always so controlled and seemed so kept together. And now, in between pathetic attempts to seduce him, she sat here bawling her eyes out on his chest. His naked chest. Hmm. She hadn't noticed that before.

She blinked the last of her tears away and became quite aware of the rapid pounding of Gabe's heart.

Maybe he wasn't as controlled as he'd have her believe.

She kept her head against his chest. "You're not immune to me, Gabe."

His hand that had been stroking her hair stilled, and then resumed its comforting movements.

"I never said I was."

"Then why—"

"Just sleep, Maddie," he interrupted, his voice gentle. "I'll stay here with you, if you'd like. But only to sleep."

Madison considered her options. Having Gabe in bed with her would be a major temptation to attempt to seduce him again. It'd be better just to send him back to his own bed. But then the thought of being alone, with the possibility of more nightmares, made it an obvious choice.

"I'd like you to stay, and I promise not to touch you. Tonight. Deal?"

He gave a soft laugh and maneuvered them so that they were lying down next to each other.

"Deal."

Chapter Five

Gabe woke with Madison's head resting on his chest. His arm lay curled around her back in a protective gesture. The light that slipped through the blinds hinted that his alarm would soon be going off, although there wasn't a clock in this room to confirm it.

He moved his hand in a gentle caress over her exposed shoulder, loving the silky texture that invited him to keep exploring her body. His hands moved to her tousled hair and he smoothed it down her back. A soft moan emerged from her mouth and his body hardened at the sexy sound.

Damn it. He shouldn't find her this desirable. Her hair was a mess. She snored. She'd even done that lip-smacking thing a couple times during the night. And he'd never been so turned on in his life. It had to be her choice of nightgown. Well, not a nightgown really. Just a tank top and white cotton panties.

"No...don't want pee'ut buttuh..." she mumbled and rolled off him onto her back, nearly pushing him off the bed.

Gabe turned to his side, propping his head up with his hand as he stared down at her. He wondered if she faked being asleep, but then she did that lip-smacking thing again. Her legs moved around on the bed, before falling open a little.

I won't look. But he couldn't stop himself. His gaze lowered to the apex of her thighs. Through the thin cotton he could see the shadow of her sex. He stared for a moment, imagining what she looked like up close. He'd touched her in the espresso shop, felt that tight, hot channel, but he hadn't actually seen it.

Knowing he was being an idiot and not much caring at this point, he reached out a finger anyway and traced it down the middle of her panties. He could feel the plump folds, and he increased the pressure of his finger until he pushed the panties inside her.

She gave a soft groan and Gabe's gaze rose to her face. She still slept.

He could feel the hot moisture against his finger and he pulled his hand away. He curled two fingers around the edge of her panties, tugging them to the side so he could look at her.

Christ, she looked enticing. All smooth, plump, and pink. He used his other hand to part her lips, groaning as he spotted the slight hint of moisture shimmering between her folds, her pink clit resting inside like a priceless pearl just begging to be sucked.

"Gabe?" she murmured, her voice sleepy and disoriented.

He jerked back. *God, if he didn't look like the biggest pervert right now.* She stared at him in confusion, then sat up and started to reach for him.

"Oh, God!" Her eyes darted to the blinds and she groaned, lurching off the bed. "What time is it? I have to open the shop! And you choose now to get horny?"

"Easy, Maddie." Gabe's gaze moved to her full breasts pushing against the thin tank top. He shifted the blanket over his erection. "I don't think you should plan on going into work today. We've got to go to the station and work with the sketch artist."

"Are you kidding me?" She turned from her action of opening her suitcase to glare at him. "This is my fourth day in business. It would be economic suicide to not keep regular hours my first week. That's the easiest way to piss off a customer. They'll think my shop is flaky—"

"Maddie." Gabe raised a hand to stop her continued tirade. "They'll understand. Just assume they saw the story on the news last night—"

"The news?" The shirt in her hand fell limp against her side. "You think this'll make the news?"

Gabe sighed, reluctant to tell her she'd already made the news. "Reporters listen to the police scanners for any hint of a story. And the Espresso Bandit is not your typical robber; he's consistent in assaulting his victims. The one before you died. And, shit, he tried to kill you last night. He'll be the top story, Maddie."

Madison sank down onto the floor and dropped her head into her hands. "I've got to call Sarah and tell her not to come in. Maybe I should put up a sign or something."

"Eric called her last night." He got out of the bed—his arousal, for the most part, subsided under his flannel pajama pants—and walked toward her. "We found her number on your desk. She was upset, but glad to hear you're okay. Eric told her to take the day off."

She gave him a despondent look—which made him feel like an ass—but he needed to stay focused.

After a moment she sighed and looked away. "I guess there's not much else to do. Do you mind if I shower before we go down to the station?"

"Go for it." He walked past her into the hallway. "I'll set out a towel and make you something to eat for breakfast."

"I don't need anything..." She sighed as he cast a warning glance over his shoulder. "Fine. I'm good with Cocoa Puffs if you've got them."

Gabe fought the urge to roll his eyes. "No. I don't have them. Damn, you women and your chocolate. Go get your shower."

Madison smiled as she walked past him and into the bathroom.

When she entered the kitchen twenty minutes later, she plopped herself down at the table with a sigh, her hair still wet and her skin all dewy looking.

He glanced away from her exposed skin down the rest of her body. "That's my bathrobe you're wearing, you realize that?"

"Is it?" Her eyes widened with mock innocence. She stood and reached for the belt tied around her waist. "I can give it back and we can finish what you started this morning."

"Never mind." He turned his back on her before she could drop the robe from her body. When she laughed, his jaw clenched. She was enjoying this a little too much. "Your bagel is ready. Do you like cream cheese?"

"Love it. You'll crack sooner or later, Gabe." He heard her pad off into the living room. "But for now I'll just watch some television."

He grunted in response and then bolted after her.

"Maddie, wait!"

But he was too late. She already stared in shock at the television set and the image of her shop being displayed.

He'd decided to check out the morning news while she was in the shower. Sure enough the media had been running the recent Espresso Bandit burglary as one of their top stories. All the local stations had sent a camera out to her shop at some point to broadcast live. It was another reason he didn't want her to go into work today. He just wished he'd remembered to turn off the news before she saw it.

"They didn't waste much time, did they?" she muttered, sinking down onto the couch.

"It's a big story. The Espresso Bandit is terrifying the coffee community."

"Yeah, that's what the reporter just said. Pretty much those exact words." She tilted her head and sighed. "Well, at least I'm getting some free advertising."

"Way to look at the positive, Maddie." His lips curved into a slight smile. "Just sit back and try to relax. Turn the channel to something more cheerful. I'll bring you your breakfast."

He went back into the kitchen, poured a mug full of coffee and put cream cheese on the bagel, and went back to the living room.

"Breakfast," he stated unnecessarily.

"Oh...is this from a coffee pot?" She wrinkled her nose at the mug. "I should have told you. I pretty much just drink espresso, but thanks. I'll take the bagel though."

The phrase *high maintenance* flitted through Gabe's mind and he shook his head.

"Coffee snob. I'm going to shower. Be ready by the time I'm out."

He left her alone with the bagel and crappy coffee.

Madison popped the last bit of breakfast into her mouth, eyed the coffee with regret, and went back to her room to change.

She pulled on a pair of jeans and a black cashmere sweater, and began searching for her socks. After a few minutes she sighed. Damn, she must have forgotten to pack any.

Her glance landed on the discarded pair from last night. It wasn't totally gross to put them on again. People did it all the time. Didn't they?

She debated for a moment before coming up with plan B. As she passed the bathroom, she could hear Gabe still in the shower. Of course he wouldn't mind if she borrowed a pair of his socks.

Madison ducked into his room and hurried over to the dresser. Sock drawer. Which one would it be? There was just one way to find out. She pulled open the top drawer.

"Hmm." She lifted up a pair of green plaid boxers and dropped them right back in the drawer. There was one mystery solved. Gabe was a boxers man.

The second drawer she hit the jackpot. At least ten pairs of blindingly white socks lay waiting. She picked up a pair and unrolled it from its perfect ball.

"*Yikes.*" Her fingers ran along the length of the sock and she found herself wondering if that whole foot and penis comparison was true. If it was, she was a very lucky girl. Or would be if he ever gave in.

She started to shut the drawer when her eyes caught a glint of silver buried under all the white. What was this? She reached in and pulled out the cold metal.

Well, well, well. Officer Martinez kept a pair of handcuffs in the bedroom, did he? Hmm. And here she'd thought he didn't have a kinky side.

These might come in handy. She grabbed the cuffs, stuffed them under her sweater and shut the drawer. She heard the shower turn off and bolted out of his room back into hers.

Her suitcase still lay open, so she threw the cuffs in and zipped it up. She had just pulled on Gabe's socks when he appeared in the doorway.

"Hi. I'm borrowing a pair of your..." she trailed off as her eyes ran down his nude—well, almost nude—body.

The towel around his waist was an inadequate fit and left little to the imagination. Madison's hand drifted over the sock covering her foot and she made the mental comparison again. She stifled a groan.

"Your socks," she managed to croak out. "I forgot mine."

His glance fell to her foot and he raised an eyebrow.

"They look a little big."

"Yes, I thought so, too."

"I just wanted to make sure you were ready. Let me throw on some clothes and we can head out."

She watched him leave, staring at his fabulous ass. It looked like granite under that towel. How could she ever have mistaken that robber's butt for Gabe's? She shivered as disgust swept over her.

Best not to go there now. She'd have enough of the Bandit issue when they got to the station. She pulled on a pair of black boots with a three-inch heel, sprayed on some perfume, and went to wait in the living room.

While Gabe finished dressing, she studied the photographs on the wall. She'd seen more photos around the house, but these were blown up to almost poster size, great black and white scenic shots. One was of a ferry on Puget Sound with the mountains in the background, another of Seattle skyline. And the last one was of a lady, who seemed to be in her early fifties, admiring the tulip fields.

The last photo drew her attention the most. The photographer had captured the spirit of this woman. She looked strong, satisfied, and at the same time resigned. The picture had been taken by someone who loved her very much.

"You ready?" he asked as he slipped a jacket on. He

followed her gaze to the wall.

"What a wonderful picture. Do you know who she is?"

Gabe opened the front door and gestured for her to leave the house before him.

She brushed past him, wondering if he would just ignore her question. It wasn't until they were underway to the station that he answered her.

"The woman in the photo was my aunt."

"Your aunt?" She really shouldn't have been surprised. When she brought up the image of the photo in her head again, the resemblance between the woman and Gabe was obvious.

"How long were you with your boyfriend?"

"Huh?" She blinked. Wow, talk about left field.

Gabe had wanted to change the subject from his aunt. With the growing curiosity about her former relationship, the question had just slipped out. "You said you were looking for rebound sex, right? How long were you with the guy?"

"Oh. A couple of years. We met in college down in Oregon. Since I moved back here, we'd been doing the long distance thing."

A couple of years? Gabe's fingers tightened around the steering wheel. Her tone had all but dismissed his question. She sure didn't sound like she was hurting over the breakup.

"What was the problem?" *Pushing, Gabe, you're pushing.*

"What *wasn't* the problem is more like it." Madison laughed. "I guess we just weren't the right fit. I can't say I'm all too upset that it's over, but still, I need a buffer between Bradley and my next big relationship."

A buffer? He'd be the buffer? Gabe tried not to feel insulted as he steered the car onto the freeway. He took a deep breath and her perfume, something spicy and sensual, tantalized him.

"Why, what are you thinking?" Her hand drifted onto his lap and slid toward the crotch of his jeans. "Are you changing your mind?"

"No." He pushed her hand off his lap, even though he wanted to open his pants and let her go at it. "What about before Bradley? Were there many?"

"Many?" She gave him a quizzical look. "Men? Women? Mechanical bulls?"

Gabe smiled. "All of the above."

"Ah." She went quiet for a moment.

Was she counting? Gabe's jaw tightened and he pushed back the jealousy. *She's not mine. She's not even sleeping in my bed. I have no right to be jealous. Hell, I don't even have the right to be asking her this.*

"No," she interrupted his thoughts. "There haven't been many. There've been a few, but not enough to qualify as many."

He could tell himself it didn't matter all he wanted, but the relief that swept through him proved otherwise.

"I mean there was Sam in high school. I lost my virginity to him," she explained. "And then there was Franco in Italy. God. Some of the things Franco taught me in bed—"

"Shit, Maddie. Enough," Gabe snapped. He didn't want to know another damn thing about Franco or Sam. Especially Franco, who sounded like some kind of Fabio-wannabe.

"Well," she shot him an annoyed glance, "you're the one who asked me. It's not like I'm asking about your love 'em and leave 'em list. I know we're short on time."

He glared at her as they pulled up in front of the station; traffic had been light and they'd made good time. "We're here. Are you ready for this?"

She looked out the windshield and her body tensed. She shrugged, but he could tell she was nervous.

"You'll be fine." He gave her hand a reassuring squeeze. "All right, Maddie, let's go."

Chapter Six

Gabe was waiting for her when she finished. She came out of the room looking tired and stressed. When her head lifted and she spotted him, her expression lightened.

"How was it?"

She shrugged and glanced back in the room where the sketch artist stood speaking with the police chief.

"The sketch she did looked almost identical to the guy I saw last night." She folded her arms across her waist and took a deep breath. "It's a little creepy. But I'm glad they have an image to get out there now."

"You did great."

And she had. She hadn't even asked him to come in the room with her. He reached into his pocket for his keys. "What do you want to do today?"

Madison gave him a surprised look. "Don't you have to work?"

"I'm off."

"You didn't have to take me down here on your day off," she protested. "You should be getting drunk or playing computer games. You know, guy stuff."

"Have you ever seen me play video games?" He gave her a skeptical glance. "Besides, I'm taking care of you right now,

Maddie. That means you're stuck with me."

Her cheeks turned pink and she glanced around as if to see if someone else may have heard.

"I'd sure like to stop by my shop and put up a sign. Would you mind?"

"Let's go. I need to get something to eat afterwards."

"How can you already be hungry? We just ate breakfast."

"You just ate breakfast," he replied. "I didn't eat anything."

"And you jumped on my ass for trying to skip it?" she demanded as she climbed into the car.

Gabe held back a groan. He had a fantastic view of her ass while it disappeared into his vehicle. Jumping it sounded pretty good to him right now.

He climbed in on his side, and then drove them out of the parking lot. She turned to him and he awaited a reprimand for his own hypocrisy about breakfast.

"Gabe." She sounded more vulnerable than accusing, and he knew she was dropping the breakfast subject. "They'll catch this guy, right?"

"Most likely. These guys don't stay on the run for very long." He didn't add that he hoped it would be soon. Because the longer the guy stayed out there, the more time he had to locate Maddie. Even if they had a sketch of the Espresso Bandit, they would still need her to identify him if he was caught. *When he was caught*, he corrected himself.

Her hands clenched in her lap. "I hope so."

The sound of a cell phone ringing broke the silence, and Madison dug in her purse to find it.

She answered, and Gabe listened to her side of the conversation. Whoever it was must have seen the news and gotten pretty upset. Madison tried to reassure them she was fine and she glanced up at him and mouthed the word *Mom* to him. He nodded.

"Today?" She sighed. "I don't know. We've been out all day. I think we're both kind of tired."

He raised an eyebrow at her in a silent question.

She covered the phone with her hand and hissed, "They want us to come to lunch today at one."

"Tell them we'll go."

"Are you sure?" Her brows knitted into a frown.

"Yes."

Madison removed her hand and accepted the invitation, then clicked off her phone.

"That's sweet of you, Gabe."

He gave her a quick glance, surprised when her hand closed over his forearm.

She stared at him through lowered lashes, her voice sincere when she spoke. "I don't know if I've thanked you for taking this—or me—on. It means a lot to me." She tightened her grip. "And I'm not saying this just because I'm trying to convince you to go to bed with me. You make me feel safe, Gabe, and I'm not sure I would have with anyone else."

Warmth rushed through him at her words, and he hated himself for it. He didn't want to be put on a damn pedestal. Sure, he thought he could protect her. But what if he couldn't?

No, he told himself. He couldn't afford to think that way. She'd be safe with him. *She would.* Nothing would happen to Madison Phillips while she was under his protection. Nothing. Unfortunately, that included sex.

Madison could see her mother watching out the window for them when they pulled up to the house a little while later.

Before they had even parked, Lillian Phillips came running down the driveway to meet them. She threw her arms around Madison and dragged her into a tight embrace.

"My poor little girl." Her mom pushed away a bit so she could look at her through watery eyes. "I just had to hold you, to know that you're alive and okay. And your face...look at that bruise!"

"I'm fine, Mom," Madison protested even as her own eyes filled with tears.

Lillian released her and reached for Gabe, drawing him into a tight hug.

"Gabriel, how can I ever thank you enough. You saved my daughter's life." She kissed each of his cheeks and heaved an unsteady sigh. "Bless you."

Gabe's face turned just the tiniest bit red, and he seemed uncomfortable with her mother's praise.

"Eric was with me," he replied. "I can't take all the credit. We were just fortunate to have gotten there in time."

It wasn't the best thing to say, because Lillian's shoulders shook and fat tears again ran down her cheeks.

"But the point is he did, Mom," Madison reminded her and drew her mother gently away from Gabe, offering him an apologetic smile.

"Yes, yes. I'm sorry I'm so emotional." Lillian brushed her fingers over her eyes to wipe away any lingering tears. "Your father is inside, Madison. He's been so worried about you as well."

"Maybe we should go in and reassure him," Gabe suggested, taking her mother's arm and turning her toward the house.

"Oh, yes, good idea. Thank you, Gabriel. You're such a

wonderful young man."

Madison rolled her eyes, not bothering to point out that Gabe was thirty-one years old. She followed behind the two and wondered if her dad would be as much of a mess as her mother was.

Thank God he seemed to have it together a little more. He gave her a quick hug, a pat on the back, and turned to offer Gabe a drink. But then, that was her dad. Always the businessman.

She followed her mother into the kitchen.

"We ordered Spaghetti Bolognese from that little Italian restaurant down the road," her mother said. "It should be here soon. Do you want a glass of wine?"

"I don't drink," Madison reminded her.

Her mother wrung her hands in front of her and chewed on her lip. "Yes, I know. I just thought with the circumstances you might want..."

"To drown out my fear with alcohol?" Her lips twisted with sarcasm. "I'll pass. Do you have any diet soda?"

"Please, Madison. You know that stuff is terrible for you. I have Perrier, if you'd like."

"That'd be fine." She took the bottle from her mother a moment later, after having declined a glass to put it in.

"Oh, Madison. That bruise looks awful." Her mother reached out and gently touched her cheek. "You should let me take you down to Cheryl at Nordstrom's. She can get you some makeup and show you how to cover it so it's less noticeable."

"I don't need any extra makeup." Madison sighed and shook her head. "It will be gone in a few days, Mom."

"Well, let me know if you change your mind. I'll treat, of course." Her mother gave her a searching look. "So...you're staying with Gabriel?"

"Yes," Madison replied and took a quick sip. "Is that a problem?"

"No, of course not," her mother rushed to say and smiled. "You know, I couldn't have asked for anyone better. I think Gabriel is a fine boy. Just fine."

Gabe followed Robert Phillips into the sitting room and took a seat in a high-backed antique chair.

"You're sure I can't get you some vodka with that, Gabe?" Robert asked, gesturing toward the tomato juice that he'd just given him.

"I'm sure. But thank you, sir."

"All right." Robert nodded. "That's one thing I've always admired about you, Gabe. You take your health seriously. I used to love watching you and Eric at those Friday night football games. You both carried that team."

"Now there's a flashback," Gabe admitted with a smile. He wondered if Mr. Phillips had been disappointed when Eric hadn't gone on to pursue college football or beyond. Robert Phillips was a supportive, dedicated man who worked hard to provide for his family.

"I hear my daughter's moved in with you."

And he was also very direct.

"That's right, Mr. Phillips." Gabe met his shrewd gaze. "Eric asked if I would watch over her until we apprehend the Espresso Bandit."

"And I agree with Eric's judgment. You're more than qualified to make sure that nothing happens to Maddie."

Interesting. Daddy can get away with calling her Maddie, but she makes a stink when I do it.

"No, I'm not worried about your capabilities," Robert went on as he paced in front of the panel window that overlooked a view of the city. "I know you realize how much I love my daughter and would be devastated if anything were to happen to her."

"Of course," Gabe agreed, sensing the message underneath the words.

"Madison's a bit fragile right now. You may have heard that Bradley broke up with her not long ago. With this new threat to her safety, I'm sure she's feeling quite vulnerable."

Gabe nodded, but wondered how well this man knew his daughter. Vulnerable wasn't a term he would use to describe her. Maybe two days ago...but since then he'd seen a solid strength in Madison Phillips that had his respect for her growing.

"I think Maddie's had enough shock. If you could keep things simple while she's with you. Don't let her do anything too extreme. She may not be thinking in a clear manner."

Gabe's attention snapped back to Madison's father and his not-so-subtle warning not to try anything with her. His annoyance level peaked, and he wanted to tell her dad to have this conversation with his daughter. She was the one into extreme seduction.

But he had too much respect for Robert Phillips to bring that up. Besides, if he could stick to his guns and keep saying no, it wouldn't be an issue.

"My only interest in Madison is keeping her safe, Mr. Phillips." Gabe downed the rest of his juice.

"I thought as much." Robert's expression held respect and something else he couldn't identify. For a moment he could have sworn it was disappointment, but that wouldn't have made sense.

The doorbell rang and Robert excused himself to answer it.

Gabe walked into the kitchen and found Madison and her mother in a deep discussion about last night's events. She glanced up and smiled when she noticed him. He returned the smile, but found himself thinking quite a bit about the conversation he'd just had with her father.

"Spaghetti's here."

They all glanced up as Robert returned carrying a silver container that must have held their lunch. Gabe gave a soft laugh. So this was why Madison ate out so much. She'd been raised this way. How could he have forgotten? Something as easy to make as spaghetti and the Phillips still ordered out.

He caught Madison's gaze again and smiled as she quirked an eyebrow at him in amusement. She must have read his mind.

She took the seat at the table next to him and whispered, "Yeah, but wait 'til you try it. This stuff is orgasmic."

Her hand ran over his thigh and he grabbed her wrist, stalling its movement. He glanced up at her dad, half expecting to find him glaring across the table, but Robert appeared otherwise occupied serving the spaghetti onto his wife's plate.

"Not now, Madison," he warned in a low voice.

"All right," she agreed and gave him an intent look. "Then later."

Chapter Seven

Later, after they'd spent the rest of the day making phone calls, closing the shop, and picking up more things from her apartment, they arrived back at Gabe's house.

"Thanks for today." Madison glanced over at him as they walked through the door. "You didn't have to do any of that. The lunch with my parents was a lot to ask. I hope that wasn't too painful."

"Of course not," he insisted, casting a sideways glance her way. "I like your family. They've never been anything but supportive of me."

"They love you." She walked past him into the living room. "I'll put in the DVD."

"All right, I'll fix us something for dinner."

Relaxing and zoning out for a few hours sounded like heaven. Anything to take her mind off the last two days. They'd stopped by the video store to make it an ultra stress-free evening.

And the post-dinner plans she had would be quite the surprise for Gabe. A wicked smile crossed her face as she grabbed the remote control and sat on the couch.

"I forgot to ask, do you eat beef?" he yelled from the kitchen.

"I do, but I prefer lean cuts."

"It is," he called back. She thought she heard him mutter something about tofu, but wasn't sure.

The sound of meat sizzling and the smell of soy sauce reached her. Hmm. Stir fry? This man could cook. Too bad he was just a rebound. A girl could get used to this.

He brought her dinner ten minutes later and sat on the couch. Sure enough, it was stir-fried beef and vegetables, with a compact ball of sticky rice next to it.

"Wow, your rice looks so perfect." She poked it with her fork and it didn't move. "How did you get it to stay together like that?"

"I cooked it in a rice cooker." He gave her an amused look as he stabbed a piece of beef with his fork.

"Right." She wasn't exactly sure what the difference was between a rice cooker and cooking it in a pot, but had no intention of asking. She took a bite and decided again how great a cook he was.

"So, what are we watching?" he asked as the previews came on.

She swallowed the bite of food in her mouth before she answered. "*The Notebook.*"

"You're making me watch a chick flick?"

"No! It's got war scenes in it, I saw it on the preview—"

"It's a chick flick," he argued and continued to eat.

"Fine. We're still watching it." She held her breath, wondering if he'd keep fighting her on it. He didn't respond. *Ha, I won.* Her smile turned smug.

When the movie ended some time later, an empty box of tissues lay on the couch and only one of them was crying.

"God, that was beautiful. To have that kind of love. I swear that is the best movie." Madison sniffled. "How can you call that a chick flick? Wasn't it just the best movie you've ever seen?"

Gabe gave her a look that said he clearly thought she was demented. "Watching that movie made me wish I drank, anything to numb the effect."

Madison rolled her eyes and jumped up from the couch. She knew her mascara had run and she must look a mess, which reminded her of the big moment she had planned. She needed to get cleaned up.

"I'm going to get changed into my pajamas. But don't go to bed, yet. I want to talk."

"Talk?" He gave her a doubtful look.

"Mmm-hmm." She avoided his gaze and hurried out of the room.

Gabe watched her go and gave a weary sigh. She seemed to be up to something, but the hell if he knew what. And maybe he didn't want to. He did know that it was ten at night and he had to be at work in eight hours.

He reviewed tomorrow's schedule again in his head. Unfortunately, he hadn't been given the okay to guard Madison when she went to work tomorrow. Another officer had been assigned to watch over her shop during the day. The thought of it pissed him off.

Round-the-clock protection had been suggested for Maddie. They had felt confident in Gabe's ability to keep her safe at night, but tomorrow she'd be in somebody else's care. Damn. She should just close up shop until they caught the Espresso Bandit. Even as he thought it, he knew the idea was ridiculous. Maddie would never do it. She wouldn't let herself be intimidated. He wouldn't do it either, if he were in her shoes.

"Hey..."

Gabe glanced up and his breath locked in his throat. Jesus. What was she trying to do to him? Her bare feet padded across the room toward him as the silk robe she wore swayed around her calves.

She sank down on the sofa next to him, curling her legs under her bottom.

"You wanted to talk?" He just managed to get the words out.

"I do." She gave him a slight smile. "I want to apologize for pressuring you into bed with me. You've been so great the past two days and all I've been doing is acting like a sex-starved nympho."

"Are you?" The words were out before he could stop them.

"Maybe," she admitted with a smile and shrugged. "But forget it. I just wanted to say sorry...and give you a kiss goodnight."

"Ah," he murmured as his gaze fell to her lips. Warning bells were ringing like crazy in his head. Just a kiss? It was never just a kiss.

"Come on, Gabe. Just one." She leaned forward, her hair falling in a curtain around her face, her lips just above his.

That kiss was beginning to sound pretty damn good. His hands circled her satin-covered waist and dragged her toward him. He slid one hand up to tangle in her hair.

"Just a kiss," he repeated and then she covered his mouth with hers. Her mouth rubbed against his in a light caress, retreating and returning many times until he couldn't take it any longer.

His tongue thrust between her lips, stroking over her teeth and into the moist interior of her mouth. She sighed and angled her head against him, bringing him deeper.

She tasted of mint, cool and sweet like she'd just brushed her teeth or eaten a mint. She grabbed the back of his neck and wrapped her tongue around his, sucking in a steady rhythm. God, he thought, the things she could do with that mouth.

He groaned and started to reach for the belt of her robe, then froze. *Self-control, get some.* He repeated the mantra in his head several times until it returned.

"Okay." He lifted his lips from hers and whispered, "There's your one kiss."

"You mean you want to stop?"

Gabe nodded and waited for her to get ultra pissed off again. Instead she surprised him by laughing in amusement.

"Well." Her lips brushed against his one more time. "I guess we'll just have to do this the other way."

Her words registered just as he heard an all-too-familiar clicking sound. He tried to push her back, but it was already too late. She had one of his wrists handcuffed and just finished securing the other cuff to the lamppost by the couch. Where the hell had she hidden the cuffs in that robe?

"I found these in your sock drawer this morning." She gave him a casual shrug.

"Maddie." He growled and jerked forward, forgetting she'd cuffed him. He jerked to a stop and fell back onto the couch. She'd chained him like a dog! How the hell had he let her get control?

"I'm going to make you a deal, Gabe." She sat on his lap and smoothed a hand through his hair.

Even though his right hand had been restrained, his left was still free. He reached up and grasped her wrist, stilling its movements.

"No. You're going to get the key out of my dresser and let me go," he ordered, his voice dropping an octave.

He knew he'd made her reconsider, because she swallowed hard and, for just a second, looked hesitant. Then she shook her head, and pried her wrist free.

"Like I said. I'll make you a deal." She climbed off his lap, as if sensing she'd be safer further away from him. She was right. "For the next half-hour or so I'm going to...entertain you. When I'm done, you can either tell me to go to bed, or you can fuck my brains out. I'm hoping for the latter."

"Let me save you the time—"

"I promise you won't say no." She stood. "Just make yourself comfortable, Gabe. I'll be back in a second."

Madison almost ran back into her room. Her pulse pounded and she even trembled while she put on her shoes. She looked in the mirror and smoothed a hand over her hair, then took a second to put on a layer of lipstick.

Enough time wasted. Gabe wasn't an idiot. He'd find a way out of those cuffs if she weren't there to monitor him. Hmm. How strong was the lamp?

She turned on the stereo in the hall and pressed play on the CD player that she already had set and waiting. The music came on and the first sensual notes of an R&B song blared. Tonight she would put those strippercize classes to use.

"Maddie," Gabe shouted from the other room. "When you uncuff me, you're not going to find a safe enough place to hide..."

She appeared in the doorway to the living room and he trailed off. She untied the belt at her waist and slid the robe off her shoulders, letting it slide to the floor. The only thing she wore underneath was a black lace bra, matching g-string, and four-inch stripper heels.

She leaned her back against the doorframe, turning her head to look at him. Her hips began to undulate, slow and steady, and his body tensed as his gaze narrowed on her. Good, she thought, he wasn't looking away.

Madison ran a hand down her neck and over a breast, stroking her nipple so that it thrust out against the lace while her hips shifted in sensual figure eights. She turned around so she faced the frame, and dragged her leg up the wall. She arched her back. With the heels on, she knew they made her legs look a mile long.

She lowered her foot to the floor and stepped away from the doorframe. Walking in a slow and deliberate advance into the middle of the room, she noted Gabe's eyes following her every step.

She stopped and pointed her foot just in front of her body, starting the slow and sensual undulations again. A smile curved her mouth as she watched him. So this was what ultimate power felt like. Gabe didn't stand a chance.

Chapter Eight

When she'd first cuffed him, Gabe had been ready to break the lamp to get free. The fact that it was an antique that had belonged to his aunt kept him from doing it. Now, watching as Madison's milky breasts rose and fell while her hips moved, he'd eagerly throw away the key.

His gaze started at the top of her head. Her hair fell past her shoulders in a sensual wave. Her gaze bore into his, full of passion and promise. It was almost too unsettling to linger there, and he dropped his eyes to her breasts. Her nipples were hard under the lace, and he could almost make out their color.

As if she knew his thoughts, she unfastened the back of her bra and dropped it to the floor. Her nipples, a tempting dark pink, hardened further, and his mouth watered. God, he wanted to taste them.

He started to rise and got jerked back to where he sat. Damn. He kept forgetting about the cuffs.

Madison gave a throaty laugh, cupping her breasts as she took another step toward him. His blood pounded and he dropped his gaze from her breasts to her navel, a tiny crater in the middle of her flat stomach. Moving his gaze further south, he let out a strangled groan.

Her movements had caused the silky fabric of her thong to slide into her folds; she looked slippery and smooth. His cock hardened and again he fought against his restraints.

"Maddie," he croaked. "You win. Go get the key and stop this."

"Stop?" She sank down to her knees on the floor a few feet in front of him. "I'm just starting, honey. I can't have you changing your mind again."

I won't. He watched as her fingers ran swirls around her nipples.

"When you touched me here..." she stared at him, "...it got me so hot."

Gabe's erection throbbed painfully under his jeans. He almost closed his eyes at the discomfort, but that would mean missing what she did next.

Madison leaned back and thrust her hips into the air in slow grinding movements. She slid a hand down her stomach to the top of her panties.

"And when you touched me here." Her voice turned husky. "It felt amazing."

Her eyes shut as she slipped her fingers below the fabric and inside herself.

Gabe choked on a gasp. He never thought he'd be jealous of a hand, but right now he would've given anything to be those fingers. Madison opened her eyes just a bit and smiled at him, her eyes cloudy with arousal.

He watched as she rolled to the side and pulled a leg out from under her, swinging it in an arch in the air as she leaned back onto her elbows. She did the same with her other leg, so she lay flat on her back with her legs in the air. Her ankles moved in slow circles, giving him the most exquisite view of her ass. She grabbed the strings on both sides of her hips and slid the panties up and over her thighs, kicking them off her legs.

They landed on the couch beside him. Her musky scent drifted up to him and he grabbed her panties with his free hand.

Madison let her legs fall back down and then open, exposing her moist folds and the cream inside. Her hand drifted back between her legs and she began rubbing her middle finger over her clit.

"You see, Gabe." She gasped as she increased the pace of her finger. "I can get myself off. But I'd much rather you do it for me."

"I'll do it. God, I'll do it."

"I know you will." She sat up again on her knees and went down on all fours, approaching him with a slow seductive crawl.

He clenched her panties in his hand, the smell and sight of her intoxicating him. The tension in him grew ready to explode and make a hell of a mess in his jeans.

Thank God she appeared to be almost done. Madison reached him, but seemed to have other plans.

She knelt before him, running her hands over the denim on his thighs.

"Get the key, Maddie," he demanded as his hips jerked toward her.

"Not just yet," she murmured and slid her hands from his thighs toward the zipper on his jeans.

He heard the rasp of the zipper and then her hands were inside, parting the slit in his boxers to find him.

"Ah, here we are." She pulled him free of his boxers and jeans, stroking him into a full erection. "The socks didn't lie."

"What the hell are you talking about?" Gabe squeezed his eyes shut, trying to slow down the orgasm that threatened to rip through him. Her hands were like satin—wait, it was moist.

God, she had him in her mouth.

Her tongue ran along the length of him, curling around the head of his shaft while her hands slipped back inside his boxers to cup his balls.

Gabe grabbed her head with his free hand and massaged her nape while she sucked at him like he was candy, moving her mouth up and down on him. Damn, she was amazing.

"Maddie, if you don't stop, I'm going to come." He grunted, his hips bucking under her skilled mouth.

She pulled back and stroked her thumb over the head, capturing the bead of moisture there. "Although I do owe you an orgasm, I'm too selfish not to get my own this time."

His hand delved into her hair. "Get the key."

She slid up his body and climbed onto his lap, reaching behind him between the cushions of the couch.

"I hid it in here," she confessed in a breathy voice as she pulled out the key along with a condom. "And this. I didn't think we'd make it to the bedroom."

"You were right." He grabbed the key from her and unlocked the cuffs, unable to believe it had been that close the entire time. Finally free, he grabbed her hips and pushed her back onto the couch, falling on top of her.

He used one hand to pin her hands above her head while he drove two fingers into her slick channel. She screamed and bucked against him. Damn. So hot and wet. He used his thumb to flick up over her clit and she squirmed.

"I'm ready, Gabe." She panted. "I don't need this."

"I do," he answered without pity and drove his fingers deeper into her. He lowered his head to her breast, tracing her nipple with his tongue. The taste of her skin was addictive. Before, he had just touched her, never tasted. He'd missed out.

His lips closed over her nipple and he drew it deep into his mouth, sucking on it in a fierce rhythm.

She cried out again and the sound of her pleas drove him wild. He pulled his fingers from inside her, rolled the condom on, and positioned himself against her tight entrance.

"Now's the part where you get your brains fucked out." Without hesitating, he thrust himself deep inside her.

Madison bowed against him, whimpering. She jerked at her wrists, trying to get them free, and he let her go. She immediately threaded her hands in his hair.

"Gabe." She gasped, her thighs clenched around his hips, her high-heeled feet in the air. "God, you feel so good. More."

He thrust into her harder, his eyes just about crossing from the sensation. He knew he wasn't going to last long, but was determined to take her with him when he came.

He found her clit again and stroked her until her body tightened against him. She shuddered, moaning out her release in a long breath. He thrust deep, pulling her tight against him. He groaned aloud when he orgasmed; the intense explosion of sensation rocking through his body.

After things became clear again, he laid his head against her breast and heard the frantic beating of her heart. Her breath came in shallow gasps.

"Wow..." Her voice came out soft and shaky. "I don't think I've ever had that kind of sex before."

Him either, but he wouldn't admit it. He nuzzled her breast before closing his teeth around one of her erect nipples and biting lightly. She moaned and held his head against her.

After a moment, he pulled himself off her. When she gave a small cry of protest, he slid his hands under her and swept her up into his arms.

"Time for bed."

"You're sending me to bed?" Her eyes widened and she looked almost hurt by the idea.

"My bed."

Her face warmed with relief and she giggled, snuggling against him. "Oh, good."

He had no intention of thinking about the consequences of what had just happened between them. It was too late. And there was no way he was going to spend the rest of the night regretting it. It had been too good, too right between them to regret it.

Plus, there were still seven hours left before he had to be at work and he planned to make good use of them.

Madison woke just before dawn. She lay on her side, her legs intertwined with Gabe's and her head nestled under his chin. She stretched, testing her body to see if any soreness lingered from their orgasm party the previous night. Between her striptease and the hot monkey sex that had continued into the wee hours, she was a little sore.

Raising her head, she glanced at the clock on Gabe's bedside table. It was five in the morning. Didn't he have to be at work soon?

Stifling a yawn, she laid her head back on his chest. A second later it vibrated under her as he groaned. His hand, which rested on her ass, tightened and his groan turned appreciative.

Madison held back her sigh of relief. She hadn't been sure what to expect from him this morning. He'd fought so hard to try to be good, and last night she'd finally broken him. She'd been prepared for anger or regret. *Something.*

"It's five in the morning, Gabe. Maybe we should get up."

His hand stroked over her ass in a gentle caress, then dipped lower between her legs to play with her. His chest bounced under her again as he laughed.

"I don't know if you've noticed, but I am up."

She moved her leg just a bit and encountered the evidence herself. He used the move to curl a finger inside her.

Madison's blood pounded at his touch and moisture pooled between her legs. She closed her eyes. *There's no way I have the energy to go another round.*

Gabe slid out from under her and eased her back onto the bed. He sat beside her, drifting a hand over the curve in her waist and up her hip.

"Tired?" he asked.

"After last night? Of course." Her body tingled.

"Well, try to rest then."

What? He gave up that easily? Disappointment stabbed through her, but then he rolled her onto her back and kissed her navel. *Ah, that's better.*

His tongue snaked out to trace around the dip.

"Just get some rest and pretend I'm not here," he murmured, his mouth moving in a slow, agonizing trail down from her belly button.

Right. She closed her eyes. *I'll just pretend this is a wonderful, delicious dream.*

His wet kisses ended at the swell of her mound, and she wondered for a second what he thought about her being bare. All coherent thoughts disappeared when his tongue swept over and into her.

Madison moaned and let her knees fall open. His tongue dragged up her folds until it found her clit, twirling around it and causing her head to spin. She bit her lip, but couldn't stop the cries that escaped her mouth.

Her response must have encouraged him, because he took her clit into his mouth and began sucking on the sensitive flesh.

Madison moaned louder as she threaded her fingers into his hair, holding him against her. She opened her eyes to look down at him. The sight of his face buried between her legs sent another pulse of arousal through her and she grew wetter.

He eased two fingers into her, moving them fast and deep while his tongue swirled around her clit.

"Gabe...oh my God!"

She threw her head back, watching the ceiling spin as her hips bucked in helpless pleasure under him. When he drew her between his teeth and thrust his fingers to the hilt, she screamed and clenched around him. Her eyes shut and color swirled behind her lids.

Her nipples hardened with the orgasm and her legs trembled from the intensity. Madison fought to get her breath back while Gabe lay back down beside her, keeping a hand between her legs and rubbing in a light caress.

"Still tired?" he murmured, kissing her stomach.

"No." She gasped and closed her legs around his teasing hand. "I'm very much awake now, thank you very much."

"Do you want me inside you?" His teeth closed around her ear and his tongue stroked over the captured lobe. "Because you are so hot and so wet that I'm going to be in a lot of pain if I don't get inside you soon."

"Do it. Now." She rolled on top of him. "Condom?"

"Drawer next to the bed." His hands moved to grab her ass while she got the condom out and placed it on him.

A moment later she raised herself up and then moved down onto his erection. Taking him inch by inch.

"You are so damn big." She moaned and closed her eyes at the exquisite sensation of having him inside her. God, he was every girl's dream. Thick *and* long. "I'm not going to be able to go to spinning class for a week."

"Spin on this." He smiled and thrust his hips upward, impaling her further onto him.

"Mmm. I love it when you talk dirty." She gasped and began her workout.

Chapter Nine

"Have a great day," Madison called after the customer who was leaving her shop.

After the lady had gone, her gaze drifted to the cop who sat in the corner reading a magazine.

"He's pretty hot," Sarah said in a low voice, following her gaze. "Man, this is fun, having some fine-ass cop hang out here all day."

It would be, if he'd been the right cop. Madison swiped at the counter with a rag. She'd been pretty disappointed when Gabe broke the news this morning. She'd just assumed that since he'd been trusted to keep her safe at night, he'd be the one to watch over her during the day.

"I think I caught him checking me out," Sarah went on after a sigh.

"Why don't you offer to buy him a cup of coffee?"

"Great idea. Why didn't I think of that?" Sarah disappeared from behind the espresso bar and headed over to the cop.

Madison laughed, surprised that Sarah had taken her seriously. She watched as Sarah said something to him and he smiled in response. Not wanting to eavesdrop, she turned her attention away and went back to cleaning.

While she wiped down the equipment, her thoughts went

back to Gabe. Gabe...and last night. Mmm. She'd done it. It was official. She'd moved into her transitional relationship and the sex was great. Scratch that. The sex was freaking phenomenal.

They still hadn't talked though. And there was bound to be some kind of post-sex conversation. What would he have to say when they sat down to dinner tonight? Doubt pricked at her. Hopefully it was something along the lines of *let's do it again and as often as possible.*

Since the robbery, she'd decided to change the hours of her shop. She still opened at six, but since business died down in the afternoon, she would be closing at four. Gabe promised he'd be the one to pick her up.

That was a good thing. Her glance went to Sarah and the cop. It looked like they were making their own plans for the evening.

Sarah came walking back with a big smile on her face.

"I take it he said yes?" Madison drawled.

"He said yes to coffee," Sarah replied as she filled up one of the ceramic mugs with the fresh brew. "And then I said yes to dinner."

"Nice. Good job, Sarah..." Madison trailed off as the cop started talking into his walkie-talkie thing. A moment later he stood and approached the counter.

"Just in time." Sarah gave him a bright smile and held the mug out to him.

He gave a bashful grin and Madison realized just how young he was. He didn't look more than a tad above the legal drinking age.

"Well, I just got a call from the dispatcher. I'm being relieved for my lunch break." He gave Madison a hesitant look and then back to Sarah. "Do you have a break coming up?"

"She's long overdue for a lunch break," Madison answered. "It's two now and the lunch rush is over. Go enjoy yourselves. I'll be fine alone."

"Well that sounds great." He nodded and hurried to say, "But I won't leave you alone, ma'am. We'll wait until my partner comes to replace me."

"Oh, right." Madison noted the looks the two exchanged and she cleared her throat. "I need to go over some of the books in the back. Can you handle things up front, Sarah?"

"Of course," Sarah answered right away and gave her a big, grateful smile.

"Great." Madison took her cappuccino and hurried to the back room. She sat in the cushioned chair and laid her head on the desk.

Watching the shy flirting going on between the two up front had her thinking again about last night with Gabe. Her head filled with the image of his head between her legs, driving her wild with his tongue and mouth. Madison groaned and crossed her legs, as if that could stop the immediate dampness in her panties.

She wanted him again. Now. But it would be a good four hours until she saw him. Lord, she was weak. She knocked her head lightly on the desk in silent reprimand.

Her thoughts turned from sex to the fact that Gabe had held out as long as he had. It was actually kind of sweet. Most men would've shelved their morals and just screwed her, especially the way she'd been throwing herself at him.

Her stomach warmed and she giggled quietly. She stood and went to turn on some music. A slow and sexy R&B song came on and she smiled. Mmm, such a sensual song. Great background music to make love to. Too bad she was missing half the equation.

Knock. Knock.

Madison snapped out of her newest fantasy and went to the back door where someone pounded. She unlocked the deadbolt, swung it open, and grinned.

"I was just thinking about you. I thought you were working." Her eyes devoured him. He was so sexy in his uniform. Was he here to talk about last night? Already? She swallowed hard. Or maybe this was the part where he said the sex was great, but it couldn't happen again? The thought had her stomach in a knot.

"You should never open the door without asking who it is, or checking if at all possible. You should get a peephole put in."

"Right. Nice to see you too." She rolled her eyes.

"I just want you to be careful. And, yes, I am working." His expression relaxed into a slow smile that had her stomach doing back flips. "But now I get to spend time with you because I'm relieving my partner."

Spend time with her? Here it came. She forced a laugh as he walked past her. "Ah, yes, the junior cop. Sarah likes him."

"His name is Brian, and he's just a couple of years younger than you," Gabe replied in amusement and walked over to her desk, placing a paper bag on top. "I brought you lunch."

She blinked, finally noticing the delicious smell. "You always seem to be feeding me, you realize that?" Madison flipped open the bag. "Soup?"

"Clam chowder."

"Oh, yummy. One of my favorites. That's sweet of you." She pulled out the bowls, set them on the table, and pried off the plastic lids. Should they go up front and eat? She hesitated. No, it appeared slow enough. Besides, the bell would ring on the door if any customers came in. "Be right back—I'll go grab us some spoons up front."

He caught her wrist as she went to walk past him, and pulled her back toward him.

"Aren't you going to say thank you?" He slid his hands down her waist to rest on her hips.

Madison's pulse skipped as he pulled her snug against him. This was a good sign, right? She licked her lips and raised her gaze to his.

"You get me so damn hard when you do that." He traced the pad of his thumb over her bottom lip and brought his mouth down on hers.

She opened her mouth to his deep, possessive kiss, willing to give him anything he wanted to take. When his tongue stroked over hers, she stroked back. His hands moved up and down her back in a gentle caress. He pulled away and touched his nose to hers in a brief gesture.

"That's more like it." He let her go.

Madison walked—a little unsteadily—to the front of the store. She let Sarah know it was okay to leave and grabbed spoons. Her mind swirled with different reactions. Gabe certainly seemed to be adjusting to the fact that they were now lovers. Did this mean no talk?

When she turned around to go back, he stood watching her from the doorway. She tapped the spoons together anxiously and gave him a puzzled look.

"I know I'm being stupid for even bringing it up," she started and then sighed. "I mean, why risk wrecking a good thing? Right? But I have to know. Have you decided to be okay with the fact that we've had sex?"

Gabe opened his mouth and closed it again, looking away from her for a moment. "Maddie...I didn't want us to have sex.

We both knew that, but it happened anyway. We can't undo it, and I'm not sure I'd want to if I could. So, here I am. Mr. Rebound." He looked back at her and gave a slow smile. "I'm done fighting it."

Confusion swept over her. Mr. Rebound? What kind of answer was that? *A suitable answer, you moron, because it's exactly what you wanted to begin with!* So it was a good thing. Right?

"Here's your spoon," she said, choosing not to respond to his answer.

He gave her a searching look as he took the spoon, and they walked back to the desk and sat.

"Anything exciting happen today?" he asked, crushing a pack of saltines into his chowder.

Relieved by the new topic, Madison smiled. "Meaning did the Espresso Bandit come by and try to knock me off? Nah. Although my business has doubled from all the publicity."

The bell at the front of the store jingled.

"See?" She raised an eyebrow and stood. "Be right back."

"You're still making the drinks?"

"Relax, I get better every day." She ruffled the top of his head as she passed.

"I'll watch from the doorway." He followed her to the front, stopping again in the doorway.

Boy, he sure was protective.

Gabe watched her swinging hips as she moved to the cash register to help the customer. His cock stirred and he had to adjust his stance. Damn, he wished his lunch hour were longer. Although she looked about as tired as he felt. A night of marathon sex had done them both in. But, damn, what an amazing night. Why the hell had he fought against sleeping with her for so long?

Because she's Eric's sister, dumb shit. And by this point with a woman, he'd usually be making up some excuse as to why he couldn't see her again. But since this was Maddie and right now she lived with him, that wasn't much of an option.

Besides, something seemed different this time around. There hadn't been the usual urge to get out and fast. No. He actually liked the idea of having her around...and having more amazing sex.

Robert Phillips' warning to not let her do anything crazy floated back to him. Guilt pricked at his conscience, but he shrugged it off. Madison was a grown woman. She made her own choices.

Maddie laughed as she bantered cheerfully with the customer, and then she waved goodbye.

"Jeez, we barely get a second to eat, do we?" She grinned and walked past him to the back room again, plopping herself down in the chair.

"I feel like some kind of celebrity," she said breathlessly, her cheeks flushed. "Maybe getting robbed was a good thing. Business has been great."

What? He narrowed his eyes, annoyance drawing his mouth into a frown. She had to be joking. "I hope you're kidding."

"Well." She blushed, but raised her chin. "I mean, of course it was a bad thing. But no amount of money could have bought this kind of advertising."

He leaned forward and looked her straight in the eyes. "He would have killed you, Maddie. That's not worth selling a few extra mochas. It's not *a good thing* that you got robbed."

"But he didn't kill me, Gabe." She folded her arms across her chest and gave him a defiant glance. "I'm fine. I've got round-the-clock protection, and soon you'll have the Bandit. If my business profits from this, I'm not going to complain."

She tossed her head and went to the doorway to look out front.

Gabe blinked, made himself count to ten. He kicked his feet up on the desk, smashing the empty chowder bowl between his hands. He tossed it into the garbage can a few feet away, his jaw tight.

"Shit, Maddie. For a while, you had me convinced that you'd grown up."

"Grown up?" She turned around, her expression taut with resentment. "I'll have you know—"

The bell dinged, signaling another customer.

"Never mind." She gave him an overly sweet smile. "I have another supportive customer to attend to. They just adore me and my shop now."

"Don't go up there without me." He jerked his legs off the desk, but wasn't fast enough. She'd already rounded the corner.

Damn it. He strode after her. He should have known better than to have gotten sexually involved with her. Maddie Phillips was still as spoiled and naïve as ever. Maybe more so.

"Gabe!"

The hysteria in her tone nearly catapulted him around the corner, just as a gunshot sounded and Madison screamed.

Chapter Ten

The first shot may have missed, but the man who stood in the entrance to the shop had raised his gun to take aim at Madison again.

"Get down, Maddie!" Gabe ordered as he pulled his own gun from its holster and put in a quick call for backup.

Madison snapped out of her frozen stupor, and finally fell to the ground so fast it was almost comical.

Gabe used the espresso counter as cover and stood just enough to where he could get off a shot. The other man had the same idea, and right after Gabe fired, a stinging heat seared across his shoulder.

The other man wasn't unscathed either. He groaned and grabbed his arm, then turned and fled the shop.

Gabe jumped up and ran after him, his feet pounding the sidewalk as he tried to keep up. But the man had a car parked near the curb, and a second later he jumped in it and squealed out of the parking lot.

"Shit." He slowed to a walk and put his gun back in the holster, then reached for his radio. After calling in a description of the getaway vehicle, he gave his shoulder a tentative roll to determine the extent of his own injury.

Very little blood and pain. It was only a graze, nothing

serious. He turned and hurried back to the shop.

Madison wasn't in sight and his heart pounded with sudden fear.

"Maddie?"

"Mmm-hmm."

Gabe followed the sound of her voice to behind the counter. She still lay on her stomach, her face cushioned on her arm. She didn't sit up or even turn to look at him.

"You can get up now. It's safe."

"I know."

Gabe sighed, not in the mood to accommodate the hysterics she might be ready to embark on.

"Do you think I'm a complete idiot?" Her voice trembled. "Because I am. I was so damn sure of myself and my own invincibility. If he had shot me, I would have deserved it."

His anger diminished some. She realized she'd been out of line. This was the Maddie he liked and admired. Gabe knelt down beside her and rubbed her back.

"You deserve a good spanking, but not to get shot. That reminds me." He glanced up at the sound of sirens.

"What?" She sat up and gave him a quizzical look. "You want to spank me?"

"No, I need to have my arm looked at."

"Your arm? Oh, God!" Madison lurched to her feet to inspect his injury. "*Oh my God!* You were shot? Gabe, you were shot! This is all my fault."

She started to babble and tears were falling. Gabe's mouth twitched with slight amusement, even if it was wrong. He watched her for another moment before trying to calm her down.

"It's a graze, Maddie." He pulled her into the curve of his good arm. "I don't even feel it. Easy, girl."

"A graze?" She hiccupped. "Are you sure? You need to go to the hospital. Now. Go get it looked at, Gabe. Please, before you bleed to death."

Gabe laughed, and before he could respond the bell above the shop rang. He gently set her aside and went to greet the half-dozen officers who'd just arrived. Brian came in behind Sarah, Maddie's lone employee. He watched as the girl rushed to Maddie's side.

"Oh no! What happened? Madison? Are you okay?"

Thankfully she had a friend to talk to now. Maddie still looked pretty shaken.

Gabe turned back to the officers and began to fill them in on the situation. Once done he turned to glance at Madison who still spoke with Sarah.

"She was lucky she wasn't shot," Brian said, shaking his head.

"Yeah, she ran out alone ahead of me. I told her not to. The woman doesn't seem to get how bad this situation is." He jerked a hand through his hair. "This is getting way too dangerous for her. Look, I need to get my arm checked out, and I want to have a talk with the sergeant. I'm going to head out. Brian, stay alert and keep her—them—safe."

"Of course," the younger man said, his hand covering the gun at his side. "Nothing's going to happen."

"Damn right," Gabe muttered and walked out the door. "I'm going to see to it."

"If I hadn't gone to lunch with Brian, maybe this wouldn't have happened." Sarah turned a frown on Madison and shook her head. "You almost got killed. Again."

"He would have shown up whether you guys were here or not," Madison replied, sipping on a latté. She'd chosen to use the decaf coffee, though. The last thing she needed was caffeine to put her any more on edge.

"Maybe." Sarah paced the floor of the shop. They'd closed early, at three. Even though they were closed, curious people kept walking by to peer in the windows to see why four police cruisers were in the parking lot.

Brian and another officer were retrieving the bullets from the wall, dusting for prints, and collecting any evidence that might be of use. They'd told her having that evidence would make identifying him even easier.

Madison glanced over at them again. Lord, she wished Gabe was still here. He hadn't even said goodbye. *Yeah*, she scolded herself, *like he'd hang around to chat sporting a gunshot wound.*

"Madison..."

She turned back to Sarah, hearing the hesitation in her employee's tone.

"I just don't know how to say this." Sarah bit her lip and looked down. "I'm too afraid to keep working here. I know that makes me sound like a total coward, and maybe I am. But I can't help it."

Madison blinked, not surprised, but unprepared to hear the words from her lone employee's mouth. What was she going to do? Without Sarah she wouldn't be able to stay open. It would take a while to interview someone and replace her.

"I love working for you, Madison," Sarah went on quickly. "But until they catch the Espresso Bandit—"

"It's all right," Madison interrupted and patted the younger girl's shoulder. "I understand, Sarah. I'll work something out."

"I feel terrible." Sarah wrung her hands and she cast a distressed glance over toward Brian. He caught her eye and gave a slight smile.

Madison watched the exchange and held back a sigh. It looked like Brian stood behind her decision, had maybe even encouraged it.

"Don't worry about it." She took another sip of her latté. "I'll have your paycheck by tomorrow."

"Thanks, Madison, no hurry. As soon as he's caught, I want to come back." Sarah smiled, looking visibly relieved. "If you still want me."

"Of course I do." Madison forced herself to smile, although she had the beginning of a tension headache.

Gabe walked inside the shop just then, his gaze determined and focused on her as he walked across the floor.

Relief and weariness swept through her body. Maybe he would take her back to his house...make another nice dinner.

"Can I talk to you for a minute?" He grabbed her elbow and pulled her into the back room.

Surprised at his abruptness, Madison struggled to keep up with him. "Hey, what's the hurry?"

"We're going out of town for awhile."

"What? Going out of town?" She shook her head. "I don't understand. Where? Why?"

"I've gotten the okay from my superiors," Gabe went on. "You're not safe here. You need to close your shop up for a week or two and I'm going to take you away—"

"Close my shop up?" she interrupted, her stomach dropping. "Hold the phone, Gabe. I just opened my shop on Monday. I will not close it again."

"Jesus, Maddie! What's it going to take?" Gabe yelled, his voice getting so loud she was certain everyone up front could hear them. He went off on some tangent, cursing in Spanish so fast she couldn't even begin to translate. Not like she spoke enough Spanish to do so anyway.

She finally just interrupted. "Gabe, you don't understand."

"No, *you* don't understand. You're acting crazy, Maddie. Listen to yourself. Do you have a death wish? Use some common sense. You need to go away for a while until they catch this guy."

Madison scowled at him and sat in the chair. Who was she kidding? She didn't have a choice. Even if Gabe hadn't been forcing a mandatory vacation on her, with Sarah quitting there wasn't any way she could stay open.

"What did you have in mind?" she asked, her tone flat.

Gabe blinked, seeming surprised by her sudden agreement. "I have a friend who owns a cabin on Whidbey Island. We disappear for a while so the Seattle P.D. can track down and find the Bandit without risking your safety."

"When do you want to leave?"

"Tonight."

Her life would be put on hold and she'd go away with him. Spending an indefinite amount of time in a cabin, on an island, with Gabe. It almost sounded romantic. Her lips twisted. Almost. But it was just business to him.

"All right." She nodded and looked around the office, reviewing the things she needed to do. "Give me a few hours and I can be ready."

∞

The ferry to Whidbey Island was a twenty-minute ride. Instead of staying in the car, Gabe convinced Madison to go upstairs and stand out on the deck.

She folded her arms on the railing and watched as they drifted further away from the dock.

When she looked to the right she could see the faint lights of Seattle. She took a deep breath. The air was different out here. Cleaner and more invigorating. Puget Sound shimmered in the moonlight, the waves slapping against the side of the white ferry.

Gabe came to stand next to her, leaning on the railing in a similar motion. He gave her a sideways glance.

"What are you thinking?"

Madison turned to look at him and shrugged. "Not much— just how beautiful it is out here. I've never been to Whidbey Island, can you believe it? I've lived in Washington my whole life and I've never been."

"You'll love it." He paused and looked back out at the water. "Are you upset about me dragging you away?"

"No." And she wasn't. She looked out over the water again. "I mean, at first I was. But it's for the best. I've decided to look at it like a mini-vacation."

"Good idea."

"What about you? Are you annoyed that you have to babysit me for awhile?"

"You're not a babysitting job, Maddie. I'm determined to keep you safe. I'll go to any lengths to do it." He heaved a sigh. "Besides, I'm being given paid leave for the gunshot wound. Don't freak out," he rushed when her eyes widened. "I told you before that it's nothing more than a graze. It's not safe for you in the city and that's why I'm taking you out of it. I *will* keep you safe."

Warm fuzzies spread through her body at his words.

"I promised your brother."

The fuzzies died a cold, hard death. Of course he wouldn't be doing this for her. He was doing this for Eric. It always came back to her brother.

He hadn't wanted to sleep with her because of Eric. The only reason he was protecting her was because of Eric. *Face it, Madison, you will always just be Eric's little sister.*

But it shouldn't have mattered anyway. He was only there for the short term anyway. That whole transitional thing she'd wanted. Right?

Her stomach felt heavy, her throat tight. All of sudden her rationalizing didn't seem so practical. She sighed deeply and shoved a piece of hair away from her eyes.

He must have mistaken her frown for something else. "We'll have him soon, Maddie. Don't sweat it."

"I know you'll get him. Especially since he was stupid enough to leave bullets in my espresso machine."

Gabe laughed.

"You shot him, though." She turned to him. "Didn't you?"

"I hit him solid in the right arm." Gabe's expression hardened. "All gunshot wounds are required by law to be reported. If he went to a hospital, we'll have him by tonight."

Madison shook her head. "He's not that stupid. I'm sure he'd sew himself up with a rusty needle before going to the emergency room."

"He came after you in broad daylight, while you were under the protection of the police. That makes him look pretty stupid in my book."

"Yeah, well he almost got me. If he'd succeeded..."

114

Gabe shook his head, his jaw going hard. "Well, he didn't. I screwed up by letting you go up front by yourself. You just aren't safe alone. Period."

"Yeah, well that's why I've got you, stud." She tried to regain the light atmosphere from earlier. "You're my own sexy bodyguard. Just like the movie. Except I can't sing and you're not Kevin Costner."

She watched the tension in his body ease again, as he cracked a smile. "Thank God for that."

The ferry started slowing as they approached the dock on Whidbey Island.

"We'd better head down to the car." Gabe straightened and took her hand. "Ready?"

"Yeah. Ready as I'll ever be," she replied and followed him back inside the ferry.

After driving for a half-hour, Gabe pulled off onto a dirt road in the woods. The road went on for a few minutes, twisting through the trees before ending at a small, secluded log cabin.

Madison looked at the view beyond it. The cabin rested on a cliff that overlooked Puget Sound and the view was something out of a travel guide. Well, if the picture in the travel guide had been taken at night. Thinking of this time as a vacation wasn't going to be so hard after all.

"Wow." She climbed out of the car and walked to the edge of the property, stopping short at the edge of the cliff. It was dark and she couldn't see much but the twinkling of lights across the water, and the shadow of the Olympic mountain range.

"I can tell you have no fear of heights," Gabe drawled from

behind her.

"Not at all." She pointed to the lights. "Where's that over there?"

"Port Townsend." His hands closed over her shoulders and he pulled her back a few steps. "You're making me nervous standing that close to the edge, Maddie."

Her toes were only about an inch away from the cliff's edge, but she allowed him to guide her back. Her thoughts were already turning to the idea of getting into bed with Gabe again. Not just for the sex, though it was a big draw, but more so for the being held afterwards. She needed a bit of cuddling after today.

Madison tucked her hand into his as they headed toward the cabin. "It's beautiful here, Gabe."

He squeezed her hand. "The inside is pretty great, too."

Madison gave him a suspicious look. "Is this the part where you tell me that this really isn't a friend's cabin, but yours?"

"What?" He looked down at her. "No, Maddie, this is not my cabin. Jesus, do you have any idea how much property like this costs?"

Madison flushed. Oh, God she was an idiot. She kept saying stupid stuff like that. In her world, where her parents owned a summer home in Europe, it wasn't improbable. But Gabe wasn't in her world; he'd made that clear before.

"I'm sorry. I guess I'm just used to that kind of *surprise it's really mine* thing because it always happens in the movies and books."

Gabe led them up the two steps to the porch. "The cabin belongs to a friend I went to college with."

Madison turned to him with a thoughtful glance.

"A lot of cops don't even have a college education, Gabe.

You have a degree in criminal justice, right?"

"Right." He unlocked the door and stepped inside.

"You don't have to settle for being a cop." She followed him into the house.

"Settle?" He gave her a hard glance.

Eek, that had come out wrong. She touched his hand. "No, wait. I'm just saying that with your degree and ability to speak Spanish, you could try for the FBI if you wanted."

"If I wanted," he agreed, flicking on the light switch. The room flooded with a soft light. "But I don't. I belong in local law enforcement. It's what I've always wanted to do. It's what I will continue to do."

"Why?" Madison asked, genuinely curious. She wanted to understand him more. To figure out what had driven him to join the local law enforcement, and what still drove him.

"Look, Maddie, I'm tired. I don't want to talk about it, okay?" His voice was rough. "Just make yourself comfortable while I go get our stuff from the car."

Madison blinked, surprise and hurt raging through her. He stepped outside the door of the cabin and left her alone.

What had just happened? He'd seemed angry at her questions. Had they really been that bad? Or maybe she had provoked it. *You just don't think, Maddie. You say things and then think about the consequences.*

And apparently she'd said the wrong thing more than once tonight. She wrapped her arms around her waist and glanced around the room.

It was just how she'd imagined a cabin would look. A lot of wood furniture with plenty of soft cushions. Simple, comfortable, and beautiful. A place to relax with someone you loved. A different kind of luxury. An absolutely wonderful cabin.

She just wasn't in the mood to appreciate it right now. Madison sat on the couch and waited for him to return.

Gabe grabbed their bags from the trunk of his car. His rush of anger had already dissipated and guilt gnawed at his stomach for snapping at Maddie. He shouldn't have been surprised that she expected him to do more with his life. The Phillips came from a different social class. They were nice people. Hell, more than nice, they'd been his second family.

But they had money and lived the lifestyle. It was what they were used to. So why was he so surprised that Maddie thought he should move up in the field? That he should want to scoot up to that higher class?

He was nothing like the Phillips. He'd grown up in poverty. When his aunt had taken him in, finances had still been tight. They'd never had fancy spaghetti dinners delivered. There were some weeks when they'd had Top Ramen five nights in a row for dinner. Hell, eggs had been a luxury.

But Martha had provided him with a good life until the day she'd died from cancer. Even after. She'd left him the only thing she'd ever owned. Her home.

He'd gone to college on a scholarship and had worked his ass off to graduate with a 4.0. He was proud of where he stood today, how far he'd come.

He might not be able to afford a cabin like this, but he wasn't on the bottom rung anymore. He'd been investing and saving, and his nest egg was looking pretty good. Of course Maddie didn't know that, seeing as it wasn't exactly something he advertised.

Be honest with yourself, Gabe. That's not the only reason you're pissed. Her encouraging him to seek a more prestigious career than being a local cop wasn't the whole reason he was annoyed. It was her delving into his reasons for becoming one. It was personal. It was painful. And he wasn't quite ready to share that with her just yet.

The only person he'd ever shared it with was Eric. And Eric was his best friend. Almost like a brother. His thoughts grew grim again. But he didn't have a brother. Not anymore.

The startled expression he'd seen on Maddie's face flashed through his head and he winced. *You dumb shit, get your ass back inside and apologize. You don't treat a woman like that. Aunt Martha would have ripped you a new one.*

When he got back to the house, Maddie sat on the couch staring at the turned-off television.

He shut the door, set the bags down, and went to sit beside her.

"I shouldn't have snapped at you."

"No, I deserved it. I'm sorry, Gabe. I spoke without thinking." She turned toward him. "I think being a police officer is a wonderful career, and I hope I didn't make it sound like I thought otherwise."

Gabe searched her eyes and saw her sincerity reflected there. "It's all right."

"I think it's a very demanding, honorable job." She paused and then waggled her eyebrows at him. "And, hey, even kind of a turn-on."

"Kind of a turn-on, huh?" Gabe smiled and took her hand.

"Mm-hmm." Madison gave a slow nod. "So here's an idea. Let's stop saying stupid things that hurt one another and do some making up."

He sucked in a hard breath as her hand slipped from his and down to the crotch of his pants.

"And I'd like to show you how much of a turn-on I think

cops are, Officer Martinez."

He heard the zipper of his jeans being pulled down, and his blood pounded at the little bit of role-play Maddie had decided to slip into.

"Please do, Miss Phillips," he managed to say as she slid off the couch and onto her knees in front of him.

She freed him from his jeans and boxers and wrapped her soft hand around his flesh. "I've been waiting all day to see this guy again."

"Really now? Take off your shirt," he commanded in a low voice and her gaze flitted up to his. "And your bra. I want to see your breasts."

"Anything you say, Office Martinez." Madison pulled her T-shirt over her head. His breath hitched as she opened the front clasp of her bra and pulled it off.

"Very nice." He reached forward to lift one heavy breast into his palm and drew his thumb across her nipple. "I love your breasts, Maddie."

"And I love your penis, Gabe," she answered with an impish grin, then gasped when he brought her nipple between his thumb and forefinger, and gave a light pinch.

"Show me how much you love it, Maddie."

"With pleasure, Officer." And her hand that grasped him started moving up and down his length. "I think we need lubrication."

Her tongue found the base of his cock, sliding over his length and up to the sensitive dent on the head. She took a moment to swirl her tongue around his throbbing head, before drawing her tongue back to the base and repeating the path again.

Soon her mouth closed over the tip of his head, and then

almost too slowly, she sucked the rest of his length into her mouth. Gabe arched his hips to push him deeper into her mouth, and she took him with ease, sucking harder and faster.

He reached out to fondle her breasts again, pinching both nipples and evoking a soft cry from Maddie. He pushed her breasts together, squeezing and kneading their plump softness.

She sucked him even deeper, until his cock stroked the back of her throat. He knew he wasn't going to last and pulled out of her mouth.

"Maddie." He groaned.

"Yes, Gabe...whatever you want."

Her invitation proved too much to resist. With her breasts still pushed together, he slipped his cock into her cleavage, moving in small thrusts against her soft flesh. She groaned and covered his hands with her own.

Pulling on her nipples, he came in quick spurts on her breasts.

"God, Maddie." He gasped, his hands massaging the milky white semen into her skin.

Madison leaned forward and kissed him while he pinched her nipples, moving his palms over the slippery flesh of her breasts. Her tongue stroked against his, and he kissed her back.

"I'm sorry. I went too far—"

"No," she interrupted. "I liked it. A lot. Please don't apologize."

"You're amazing, Maddie." Gabe closed his eyes. And she was. How the hell had he gotten this lucky?

Madison stood and offered a delicate shrug. "Besides, I owed you an orgasm, remember?"

"Ah, how could I have forgotten?" He laughed and shook

his head.

She yawned. "I think I'm going to shower and get ready for bed."

"There's only one bedroom. If it's a problem, I can take the couch."

"A problem?" Madison gave him a chiding look. "A benefit is more like it. Will you join me soon?"

"Of course."

"All right." She yawned again and leaned down, pressing her lush lips against his. "Thank you again for everything, Gabe."

"Thank you." He tucked a wayward strand of hair back behind her ear and murmured, "And anytime, *mi vida.*"

Chapter Eleven

Madison put the cap back on the toothpaste and looked up, staring at herself in the mirror. The memory of the erotic moment they'd just experienced ran rampant in her head. That and the fact that he'd just called her *mi vida*. Didn't that mean *my heart* in Spanish or something? *Whatever, Madison, it doesn't mean anything.* He was just being sensitive and a good friend. *Right. Good friends call each other* mi vida *all the time.*

And why did it evoke images of old television reruns, shows in black and white that her parents had grown up on, where couples were in love, and the men called their women sweetheart. Or maybe it was darling, but in either case...it was the same idea.

Madison groaned. *Why am I doing this to myself? Why am I trying to make this romantic and sweet? It's sex. It's nothing more than sex.* She brushed vigorously, taking out her frustration on her teeth.

She finished and set her toothbrush on the counter, then looked back in the mirror and raised a finger to the image.

"You will not make this into something it's not," she whispered with a fierce scowl to herself. "It's sex. Damn good sex. But nothing but sex. So get over it, sister."

Satisfied with her self-administered pep talk, she pulled off the rest of her clothes and climbed into the shower.

Gabe finished typing the email to Eric and hit send. He'd informed Maddie's brother of what had happened this afternoon and the change in plans. He didn't specify where they were, but guaranteed her safety. Her parents were more than likely beyond freaking out by now.

With that out of the way, he took care of some other needed online business and signed off, then went to prepare for bed. He couldn't stop thinking about what Maddie had let him do to her a few minutes ago.

Gabe shook his head. She revealed different layers of herself to him every day. And this was the same woman who'd just handcuffed and performed a striptease for him the night before. He shouldn't be surprised by anything she did.

The more he thought about their intimate moment in the living room, the more eager he became to climb into bed with her.

When he opened the door to the bedroom, the light from the hall shone a beam onto Maddie's sleeping form. She lay on her stomach, with her cheek turned on the pillow toward his side of the bed. She was fast asleep.

His gut tightened at the image she made. So vulnerable and beautiful. His desire subsided. The desperation and urgency hit him then. He would do anything to keep her. A vow to protect her resonated again in his mind, pounding a silent mantra while he took off his clothes and climbed naked into bed beside her.

He ran a hand over her back and paused to massage the soft curves of her bottom. She had gone to bed in panties and a tank top again. It seemed to be a favorite of hers for bedtime attire. And he loved it.

Gabe pulled the panties down, so he could look at her. The

firm globes of her bottom popped free and his palms slid to cover them. He kneaded them and moved his thumb up and down her crack.

"Mmm." She stirred, and lifted her ass further into his hands. "You decided to join me."

"Like I could resist." He moved his fingers back down and probed the hot moistness between her thighs.

She moaned and wiggled against him, opening her thighs wider. He started to finger her until she grew hotter, wetter, and she squirmed on the bed.

"Gabe...you're teasing me."

"You like it." He reached underneath her to squeeze her breast.

"Yes. But I like other things too." She giggled and then groaned when he rubbed her clit.

He pulled her panties all the way off her body. "All right. Why don't you get up on your hands and knees, *mi vida*."

Maddie struggled to pull herself up, shrugging off her tank top at the same time. She moved onto her hands and knees as he'd requested.

"I like the sound of that."

His gaze lowered to her sex, shiny with moisture. *So do I.* He grabbed a condom out of the bedside table and put it on.

He grasped her hips and probed the slit of her sex with the head of his cock. Taking a deep breath, he pushed inside her, slow and steady. Her inner muscles tightened around him, her liquid warmth welcoming him.

"Oh God." She pushed back against him, sending his cock deeper. "You feel so good."

"I was going to say the same thing." He pulled out and thrust back inside.

He reached in front of her to cup her breasts, which bounced with each thrust. She moaned as he plucked at her nipples, bringing them to their full length.

Gabe started pounding into her harder. Maddie's cries turned to screams, and her body clenched around him. The sensation drew a ragged groan from him and sent him over the edge. He came hard, squeezing her hips and thrusting until he had fully spent himself.

Madison's knees gave out and she fell forward with a sigh. Gabe pulled out of her and lay down beside her, kissing her shoulder and nuzzling her neck.

"God, you are sexy, *mi vida.*" He nipped at the nape of her neck, loving the saltiness of her damp skin. "I'm sorry I woke you up."

"Don't apologize," she replied, drowsy again. "It was a helluva way to wake up."

Gabe smiled, nuzzling her neck again before he closed his eyes. God, she was an incredible woman.

Madison opened her eyes the next morning and realized Gabe's head was just an inch away from her.

She smiled and sat up. His arm slid off her back where it had been resting. He lay sleeping, but the dark circles under his eyes showed that he hadn't been getting enough.

She climbed off the bed, hoping he would stay asleep. She watched his brows draw together in a slight scowl, but he didn't stir.

Once out of the bedroom, Madison headed straight for the kitchen. It was time to repay Gabe in the cooking department. Biting her lip, Madison glanced into the somewhat stocked fridge. Someone must have been here not too long ago because there were eggs and milk that hadn't yet expired.

She pulled the eggs from the fridge and began searching the kitchen for bread. When none could be found, Madison grabbed the box of pancake mix she'd seen earlier and opened the freezer. Aha. Chocolate chips. Gabe might not need a chocolate fix, but she sure did.

Especially when she was also being deprived of her morning latté. They were going to have to find an espresso stand sometime in the next couple days. One day, she could handle. Two days and someone would get hurt.

Ten minutes later she was in the midst of flipping a pancake when Gabe walked in. The stunned look on his face made it difficult not to smile.

"You're making breakfast?"

"Yeah, the eggs are almost ready," she replied and slid the pancake onto a plate beside her.

Gabe's glance slid to the stove and he frowned. He must have been looking for the frying pan.

"Not there. There." She jerked her head to the left just as the microwave dinged.

His eyebrows drew together and he opened his mouth to say something, but then shook his head. Instead he walked over to the microwave and opened the door, pulling out the steaming bowl of scrambled eggs.

"What, you've never microwaved eggs before?" She took the bowl from him and dished out equal portions onto two plates, and divided the remaining pancakes between each plate.

"I can't say that I have."

He cleared his throat, and looked down at the plate, obviously hesitant to try it.

"You should. It's so much quicker. Just be careful not to

leave them in too long or they start exploding." Just then there was a popping sound and the scrambled eggs shifted on his plate. "See, like that. Have a seat."

Gabe sat, sliding his chair toward the table. He stared at the plate in front of him. Did people really microwave their eggs? Why, when they were so easy to make on the stove?

"Do you want syrup and butter?" She waved a hand. "Never mind, I'll bring them out, because I do."

She went to retrieve them and came back a moment later, setting the syrup, butter, and a bottle of ketchup on the table.

"Ketchup?" Gabe raised an eyebrow. What the heck did she need ketchup for?

Madison grabbed the bottle and flipped open the lid. "I like them on scrambled eggs."

He watched as she squirted a glob in the middle of her microwaved eggs, holding back a shudder. He would never have picked her for a ketchup-on-eggs type of girl. Shaking his head, he decided to try the pancake. He wasn't avoiding the eggs—he just wasn't quite ready to try them yet.

The pancake couldn't be bad. It looked like she'd even found some blueberries. He took the first bite and stopped chewing.

"Are these...chocolate-chip pancakes?" He forced himself to swallow the ultra-sweet concoction.

Madison glanced up from her task of drenching her pancake in syrup. "Yeah, do you mind? I guess I could have made some plain."

"No, this is fine," he heard himself say, and then it hit him. He was in way over his head.

He sat here eating microwaved eggs and chocolate-chip

pancakes, for God's sake. He could have refused her breakfast in a polite way, come up with some excuse. Instead he shoveled it in and grinned like it was a five-star meal.

"You like it?" Madison responded to his smile, looking happy with herself. "You should let me try dinner sometime. I can do the most creative things with chicken."

"I'll bet you can." He forced a bite of egg and immediately realized why she used ketchup. He moved his teeth back and forth over the rubbery eggs until they were chewed up enough to swallow. "But you're treating this time here like your vacation, so I should do the cooking. You relax."

"Yeah." She waved a fork at him. "But I got you shot yesterday. It's the least I can do."

"Grazed, it's just a graze." He forced himself to keep eating. "Do you want to go for a walk on the beach after breakfast?"

Madison glanced up at him, her eyes shining like he'd just offered to take her to Paris.

"That sounds great. I need time to shower and put on makeup—"

"Skip it," he interrupted. "You can take a long bath tonight. You'll need it more later. Just throw on some jeans you don't mind getting dirty and a T-shirt. Pull your hair back in a ponytail, and you don't need makeup."

"I don't know." She shrugged. "Bare-faced in the morning is okay...but as the day goes on, it's not pretty."

"Oh, please." He stood, having managed to eat more than half of the breakfast, and took his plate to the sink. "You're gorgeous and you know it. With or without the makeup."

The room went dead silent, and he turned to see what he'd done wrong. She stared at him with wide eyes, her mouth parted in a smile of amazement. It was a look that broke all the rules, one that said the word rebound might once again just be a basketball term. The thought struck a strange note inside him and he turned back to the sink.

"Why don't you go get ready when you're finished eating and we'll head out. Wear a bathing suit under your jeans if you brought one."

"I did." Her voice sounded different, as if she too were aware of the subtle change that had just occurred.

When she'd left to go change, he wondered why a conversation about makeup had altered things. But that was stupid. It had been about more than that. Nothing about their relationship had been casual since that first sexual encounter in the coffee shop. Add to that the fact that he'd saved her twice from being killed, and things got even more complex.

Gabe shook his head to clear his thoughts. Turning from the sink, he dried his hands on the kitchen towel and went to grab some things for the hike.

Madison shrugged into a wool zip-up hoodie and glanced at herself in the mirror. *No makeup.*

She tilted her head and looked at her profile. It wasn't so bad. Maybe she could do this natural thing more often. *Or maybe that pretty flush in my cheeks is due to Gabe.*

Madison smeared on sun block and applied lip balm. Technically they weren't makeup, but still a necessity.

Gabe was waiting for her in the living room, looking mighty fine in his snug jeans, with a backpack slung over his shoulder. Mr. Hottie-Hiker himself.

"Ready?"

"Hmm, maybe you should define ready." She smiled, raising an eyebrow as she walked past him to the door.

He gave a soft laugh and followed.

Madison stopped on the porch, realizing she had no idea where they were going. She turned, waiting for him to take the lead.

"All right, Maddie, I hope you're ready to get dirty." He stepped off the porch, striding toward the edge of the cliff.

She smiled and hurried after him.

"So where are we going to hike anyway?" It almost seemed as if he was going to go right over the edge, but then he veered away from the drop and began walking parallel to the edge.

"Down to the beach."

After a few minutes she saw it—a trail that weaved down the side of the cliff.

"The trail is steep, so watch your step." He turned back around to look at her. "I'll go slow, just let me know if you need to stop."

"I'll be fine," she assured him and watched as he jumped over the edge and down a foot onto the trail.

He turned and offered his hand to help her over the slight drop. She glanced down at it and then placed her hand in his. The now familiar tingle shot up her arm when they touched, but she forced herself to ignore it and instead concentrated on getting her footing.

She released his hand the moment she had her balance and gave him a wide smile. "Ready when you are."

"Let's do it."

Madison hurried to catch up with his brisk stride. The first half of the trail wasn't very steep, but wound down the cliff in a gradual horizontal decline.

They moved at a steady pace for a good half-hour and she barely broke a sweat. It was the last five minutes of the trail that were the real challenge.

Gabe stopped, looking back to check on her. "Okay, you probably guessed, but that was the easy part. We're almost down, but this last bit gets tricky."

Madison glanced at the hillside that seemed mostly sand and rock. A pretty serious incline. She worried her lip. How primitive. Why hadn't someone built some stairs down to the beach?

"So how do you go about getting down?"

"Small steps," he answered as he began the descent.

She watched him for a moment, seeing how he did it. His steps were small, but still quite fast. That whole *run so you don't fall on your face* method.

If I try that I'll end up on my face. She took a deep breath and set out. Gabe reached the bottom before she'd even taken five tiny steps.

Her tennis shoes slid in the sand and she cursed, reaching out to grab a shrub on the side of the trail.

The sound of Gabe laughing rose up to meet her and she glared down at him.

"Glad that you're getting some amusement out of me just about falling on my ass," she yelled and took another couple steps.

"You're doing fine, Maddie," he called, looking apologetic. "Baby steps, just take baby steps."

Just when she thought she had the hang of it, her shoe skidded in the sand again and this time she did land on her butt.

She sighed. Well at least she'd taken his advice and worn some old jeans. She started to try to stand back up, but then stopped.

"Screw it," she muttered. "My jeans are already dirty. I'm doing this the easy way."

She sat back down on her butt and slid the rest of the way down. Gabe helped her up once she'd reached the bottom, a huge smile on his face.

"You did great."

"I came down on my ass." She shrugged. "But it worked."

Even though she had made it to the safety of the beach he didn't release her hand. "Hey, as long as you made it down, who cares, right?"

"Right, that's what I figure. Although I'm afraid of what my butt looks like right now."

Gabe stepped around behind her, taking in the view for himself and gave a wolf whistle.

"You look pretty damn sexy, *mi vida*. But you have a little dirt here..."

Madison focused on the hand that smoothed over her denim-clad bottom, instead of the fact that he'd called her *mi vida* again. The hand was a pleasant distraction.

His fingers gave her ass a light squeeze as he leaned forward and kissed the back of her neck.

She moaned and leaned back into him. "Mmm, so the hike was just an excuse to have sex on the beach?"

"Yeah, get naked."

Madison giggled, closing her eyes as his teeth closed over her earlobe. She squirmed as heat flooded through her. "Isn't this a public beach?"

"Of course."

"Would we be breaking the law?"

"I'm off duty, don't ask." He stepped back. "But let's go for a walk first. The low tide doesn't last for more than a couple of hours."

When his hand disappeared from her backside, she felt a pang of disappointment. But it went away as soon as she turned to at last observe their surroundings. She stared in amazement, taking a deep breath of air that smelled salty and like seaweed.

"It's so beautiful down here." She looked down the beach in both directions and out over the Sound. "And seeing the mountains in the daytime is like a hundred times more amazing."

"I thought you'd like it." He gave her a sideways glance as he unzipped his backpack.

"I love it."

Puget Sound lay still since there was no wind to create whitecaps. Clear and shimmering near the beach, a few feet from shore, the water became a dark blue and all visibility below the surface vanished.

Her gaze followed the vast body of water across the way until it was broken by Port Townsend and the Olympic Peninsula. The mountains that jutted up from the peninsula took her breath away.

"Have you ever been camping?"

"Nope." Madison shook her head, not wanting to look away from the view.

"The Olympic Forest over there is a great place to go camping."

She stared in amazement at the mountains, a smile playing on her face. Her parents hadn't been the camping type, more like the Hilton in Switzerland type.

Although Eric had gone camping with Gabe many times.

They'd made it an annual summer tradition during high school. Madison had often wondered what it would have been like to go along, had even envied them a couple of times.

The sound of a click and a whir brought her out of the memory. She turned to look at Gabe, surprised to find him holding a camera.

"What did you take a picture of?"

"You." He wound the camera. "Do you mind?"

"Nah, I'm not one of those people who freak out about getting their picture taken." Then she remembered she wasn't wearing makeup. Oddly enough, it didn't bother her.

She looked at the camera in his hand. It wasn't a little disposable thing, or a digital, but one of those ultra expensive-looking ones that you had to do all the work on and develop the pictures the hard way.

"Do you take a lot of pictures?"

He shrugged and turned the camera to the mountain range. "It's just a hobby."

Madison noticed his intensity as he continued to take pictures. A memory floated through her head—the photo of his aunt that hung in the house. She gave a small nod of understanding.

"You took that picture. The one of your aunt. And all the other ones hanging in your house."

"Yup." He didn't look at her, but continued to take various shots of water and mountains.

"Would you consider letting me sell some of your pictures in my shop?"

That got his attention. He lowered the camera and turned to face her.

"I don't take pictures to make a profit."

"I know you don't, Gabe." She gentled her tone. "I'm not implying that you do. Your photos are wonderful and I think you should share them with the rest of the world. What's the harm in letting me sell a few in my shop? I like to promote local art."

"I don't know, Maddie." He went back to taking pictures.

"Well, if you don't want me to sell them, would you at least consider letting me have some to decorate with?"

He took a moment before giving a slow nod. "I'll think about it."

"That's all I'm asking, sweet cheeks." She gave his butt a nice squeeze in retaliation from earlier. "Are we going to keep walking, or should I make myself comfortable for a while?"

"Damn, you're impatient," he muttered, although he still smiled.

She bit her bottom lip and nodded, a smile lingering on her face. "For more than you know."

He returned his camera to his backpack and took a step toward her. "The longer we wait, the better it'll be. I promise."

"I know." Her lower lip jutted out. "I'm just not a patient person when it comes to having you inside me."

Her words had an immediate effect on him, and Gabe felt himself stir inside his jeans. She was flirting, making it no secret she wanted him, but still he stuck to his guns in telling her to hold off. He told it to himself as much as her.

She was casually dressed, sweaty from the first part of their hike, and he'd never found her sexier. Maybe it was the two braids she'd done her hair in. It brought up all kinds of kinky thoughts.

He rubbed his thumb over her lower lip that pouted in such

an enticing way.

"Trust me, I'll make it good."

"Mmm, I bet you will." Her tongue reached out to draw his thumb inside her mouth. "Are you ready?"

"Ready?" All thought scattered from his head, and his entire focus turned to her moist mouth moving over his thumb.

She released his thumb and drew back. "To hike down the beach?"

"Right. The hike." He nodded like an idiot. God it was amazing how quickly he could lose control of the situation. "Let's head on out."

She winked at him as he turned and once again led the way.

Chapter Twelve

They walked about a mile down the beach before he steered them off the beach and onto a barely noticeable trail in the forest.

"What's back here?" Madison asked, wiping away the sweat from her forehead. She was hot and sticky, and hoping that Gabe had told her to wear her swimsuit under her clothes for a reason.

"About fifteen minutes into the forest there's a great lake to go swimming in." He glanced back at her. "If you don't want to swim we can just do the picnic lunch."

"Oh, I'm swimming." She grinned. "I think I'm wearing half the sand from the beach."

They kept walking and soon she saw the shimmer of a greenish-blue lake. She gave a yelp of excitement and pushed past him to run ahead.

When she reached the opening of the trees, she looked over at the picnic area. It must have been a place people came to, because there were picnic tables and fire pits around.

"I love it!" She looked over at Gabe, who now stood beside her. "Is this only accessible by hiking in?"

"No," he admitted. "There's a back road most people don't know about. But the hike makes it that much better."

"No kidding." Madison walked to the picnic table and sat, sighing as her feet started to tingle. "That was a great hike, but my feet are about ready to fall off."

"And just think." Gabe set the backpack on the table. "We get to do it again on the way back."

She raised an eyebrow. "I can handle it. But I plan on staying here for at least an hour, with or without you."

"With me. This is my time to play too." He pulled off his T-shirt, exposing his hard chest.

Madison had to lift her gaze from the taut muscles there, to his shoulder and the jagged red line on it. Her insides twisted as she remembered how he'd acquired it.

"How's the bullet woun—graze?"

"It's fine. Forgot I even had it," he assured her and unzipped his pants.

She laughed. "Whoa there, boy. Give a girl a chance to catch her breath."

"Catch your breath, *mi vida*." He jerked the jeans off his legs and stood in front of her in his boxers. "I'm going swimming. Are you sure you don't want to come?"

"No, I do. Actually, nothing sounds better than cooling off right now. I'm sweating like a pig." She grinned and unzipped her sweater.

"Good choice." Gabe walked over to his backpack and pulled something black and shiny out of it.

"What's that?" Madison asked as she shrugged out of her shirt and jeans.

"Plastic inner tube."

She watched as he went to work blowing it up. Although he seemed focused on getting it inflated, his gaze followed her while she undressed. His eyes darkened when she had finished and stood before him in her bikini.

Madison held back her smile. Hmm, so he liked the red string bikini, did he? Good thing she'd thought to pack it on the trip to Whidbey.

But what was the inner tube for? "I'm a pretty good swimmer. I don't think I'll need that."

He raised an eyebrow and kept blowing. When the tube had been fully inflated, he plugged up the air hole.

"You might find yourself surprised. All right, let's go."

He grabbed her hand and she giggled, running after him as they made for the water. Gabe tossed the tube out a few feet and dived right in.

He emerged a few feet out, gasping as drops of water dripped from his face and hair.

Hmm, it looked a little cold.

"Are you coming or what?" he called out, treading water.

"I'm coming." Madison didn't hurry, but toed her way in and winced at the coldness of the lake. They had to be nuts to be going swimming, it was only May and barely seventy degrees outside.

Gabe swam back to the shore and stood, wading toward the lake's edge.

"It's colder than I thought, Gabe." She hesitated. "Maybe I'll just wade."

"What?" Before she could reconsider, Gabe had grabbed her around the waist, carried her a few feet out and tossed her under.

She came up sputtering, goose bumps covering her skin and her teeth chattering.

"Maybe I'll just wade," he mimicked. "Come on, Maddie. You're not getting off that easy."

140

Madison swept her palm across the water and doused him with a spray of water.

"That was so not nice! It's freezing in here!" she grumbled, but ruined her mock anger with a laugh.

"Ah, you want me to be nice?" He took a step toward her.

She shrieked, and dove under the water, emerging a few feet out, before swimming further away.

He laughed and swam after her.

The water temperature didn't seem as bad after awhile. Either that or she'd gone numb.

Madison reached the inner tube and clung to the edge. She'd gone out at least twenty feet or so from where she could touch the bottom of the lake.

A hand wrapped around her ankle, and she screamed as she was dragged backwards and underwater.

When she came up for air, Gabe had taken her place.

"You said you didn't need it." His eyes twinkled with mischief. "But if you're nice, I may share."

"I can be nice," she murmured and sighed as he grabbed her wrist and pulled her close.

"Can you?" He lifted the tube over their heads and dropped it back down so that they were in the hole in the center of the tube.

Madison spread her arms out on either side of the tube, holding herself up as she tread water. Gabe tossed one casual arm around the float and gave her a slow smile. They were so close together that her legs would scissor in-between his every few moments.

"I have this fantasy," he began, and toyed with the string on her bikini top. "That I read in a book. It involved water, a man and a woman, and a flotation device."

"Sounds interesting." Her gaze skimmed to the beach to confirm they were alone. "Wanna tell me about?"

"I'd rather show you." Gabe's nimble fingers untied the knot behind her neck, and the strings fell down onto the fabric that still covered her chest. "Damn, that's what I love about your breasts. You don't even need the top to hold them up."

Madison laughed even as heat spread through her body. "I think it's only fair that I remind you we're in water. The buoyancy factor helps."

"They're great on land, too." He pulled the red top down off her breasts, but didn't remove it all the way.

She caught her breath when he used the palm of his free hand to rub over the sensitive tip of her breast.

"Is this a popular lake?" she asked, more than ready to go at it, but also worried about the chance of being discovered.

"Very popular."

He let go of the tube and his body sank in the water a bit, bringing his mouth level to her nipple. When his teeth closed over it, her eyes shut and she groaned. Sparks of pleasure made their way from her breast to the sensitive spot between her thighs.

Madison moved her legs faster in the water, as if the movement could release the throbbing of her sex.

"Don't tell me you've never had sex in a public place before?" He drew her nipple deep into his mouth and started sucking.

"Ah." It was starting to be hard to stay afloat. "Does masturbation count?"

His mouth stopped moving, and he looked up at her with a startled glance.

"Never mind." She groaned and pushed his head back to

her breast. "Please, don't stop."

"Right." His tongue swept against the peak of her breast and he drew it between his teeth.

"Gabe." Her nails dug into the rubber of the tube and her eyes started to lose focus. Just as fast, they regained focus on the car that bounced through the forest toward the lake. "Gabe! Stop, oh my God, there's someone coming."

Gabe lifted his head and looked toward the shore. He pulled her bikini top back into place and tied it around her neck.

"Should we go back?" Madison asked. Frustration and disappointment clawed at her belly. Damn, it just figured they'd get interrupted.

"Maybe, maybe not." Gabe gave a casual wave to the couple who had just climbed out of the car and were looking out at them.

"Do you know them?"

"No." He shrugged. The couple waved back and then began setting up a blanket under the trees. "But they look pretty cool."

"What do you mean? You're not going to ask them to join us or anything?" Madison raised an eyebrow, trying to figure out his line of reasoning.

"Of course not." Gabe reached down and grabbed her legs, wrapping them around his waist. "They can't see much. Just from the shoulders up."

He held onto the float with one hand and kept treading to keep them both just above the water.

"They don't care about us anyway, trust me." He lowered his head and closed his mouth over hers.

Stop this. Madison knew she needed to, her conservative upbringing told her to. But the fingers Gabe slipped into her bikini bottoms encouraged her otherwise.

"Gabe," she breathed against his mouth, her thighs clenching around his waist.

"Yes, *mi vida.*" His hand cupped her sex, giving it a light squeeze as he smoothed a finger back and forth over her exposed folds.

"This is crazy. I'm so turned on right now."

"Even though we're in water, I can tell." He pushed the finger deep inside her and moved it in a slow circle. "Because your wetness is different than the lake. It's hot, silky and smooth."

She lost the ability to respond as he pinched her clitoris and began stroking it. Her head started to roll back onto the float, but she caught herself just in time. *Try to appear normal in case the couple on the beach is watching.*

The last thought made another pang of arousal shoot between her legs. Her heart pounded faster. She liked it. The thought of being watched.

She lowered one of her hands under the water and delved into Gabe's boxers to find his erection.

"You're so hard." She encircled his width with her hand, and moved her palm up and down the length of him.

"I don't need a reminder, *mi vida.*" He groaned and removed his hand from her bikini to push his boxers down to his knees. "I can't wait anymore."

"I'm not asking you to." She clenched her inner muscles around the fingers that were working inside her.

He reached down and untied one side of her bikini bottoms, pushing it aside and leaving open the cleft that he sought. Slowly, with her legs still wrapped around him, he pushed into her.

144

Madison inhaled sharply at the increasing pressure. This time her head did fall back and she didn't give a damn.

Gabe moved slow and deliberately, seeming careful not to disturb the water around them too much. When he had embedded himself to the hilt, he began to withdraw and press right back in.

"You're amazing." She lifted her head and met his steady gaze.

"So are you, *mi vida*. Not to mention you're my fantasy come to life." He rocked his hips just a bit, causing him to wedge near her cervix. Madison clenched her muscles around him and his breath hissed out.

"Keep doing that and I'm not going to last much longer."

She squeezed again, pleased at the power that she had over him right now. "That's all right. You'll just have to go another round tonight then."

He withdrew again, moving his hips in a way that he hit a spot in her, making her suddenly buck on him.

"Good spot?" He grinned.

"Is that what the G stands for?" She gasped, and he rewarded her again by stroking that sensitive area. This time her body clenched on its own accord and the orgasm that ripped through her took her by surprise. Pleasure spiraled through her, lights flashed behind her closed eyes.

"I guess so," he answered and increased the pace of his steady thrusting. She still lay weak when he came a moment later.

Her gaze drifted to the beach with mild guilt. Relief took its place when she saw the couple deep in conversation with each other, oblivious to what was going on. Well, she hoped they were oblivious.

She unwrapped her legs from Gabe's waist and fumbled to tie her bikini back in place.

"Here, let me." He disappeared under the water and a moment later she felt him lightly bite her inner thighs.

Before she could even acknowledge it, he stopped and turned all business, tying her back into place. He emerged a second later.

"Want me to help you with yours?" she offered with a grin, but he stopped her before she could submerge beneath the water.

"I already took care of it."

His tone had cooled considerably, and Madison gave him a closer look. He wouldn't even meet her gaze.

"We should get out and head back." He ducked out from the center of the tube. "We have a long hike ahead of us."

Madison blinked, feeling abandoned as she tread water alone in the center of the tube. "I thought we were going to have a picnic."

"Right." He glanced toward the shore. "We can if you want, I just have some things—"

"No, never mind." She abandoned the tube and swam toward the shore, eager now to get away from him and whatever had soured his mood.

She reached the shore just a few seconds before he did. But soon he'd passed her in his haste to get dressed and pack things up to get ready to go. The other couple waved goodbye as Gabe and Madison headed back onto the trail.

They made the hike back down the beach in silence. Madison made sure to stay at least a couple of feet behind him. She wanted to be as far away from his short fuse as possible.

What happened? She kicked loose rocks into the Sound

every now and then as she analyzed the time from arriving at the lake until the point they left. She came up with nothing.

When they reached the bottom of the cliff they needed to climb to get back to the cabin, she couldn't take it anymore.

"What's your problem, Gabe?" she blurted. "What the hell happened? Was it something I did?"

He didn't answer, just began making his way up the rocky incline.

"You don't think I deserve an answer?" she shouted, hurrying to catch up to him so he couldn't ignore her. "You're being a freaking—shit!"

She lost her footing and fell, sliding back down the few feet she'd just climbed. She reached out to halt the unwanted descent and managed to stop herself. Not without the price of tiny rocks cutting into her palm, though.

Tears filled her eyes, more so from the frustration with Gabe than the pain. She made no move to get up, but he was already backtracking to get to her.

"Damn." He reached down to help her up. "Are you okay?"

"What, like you care all of a sudden?" she snapped, willing the tears in her eyes to go away.

He took her wrists in a gentle grip and turned them over so he could examine her palms.

"You're bleeding."

"It's just a scratch." She tried to pull her hands back, but he held fast.

"Here, let me rinse the dirt off." He pulled off his backpack and took a bottle of water out of the side compartment. After unscrewing the cap he doused her minor wounds with the water. "I'm sorry, Maddie."

Relief that he had apologized made the tension leave her

147

shoulders and she just nodded instead of answering. She watched the dirt rinse away from her hands, leaving only the tiny red cuts.

Gabe screwed the cap back onto the bottle and sat beside her. For a moment neither of them said anything. He turned to look at her and picked up one of her hands.

"Are you going to tell me what happened?" she asked softly. "Why you shut down on me?"

Gabe hesitated and then sighed. "We got a little carried away back at the lake. We weren't thinking." When she looked at him with no sign of understanding, he spelled it out for her. "We didn't use protection, Maddie. I realized it when I pulled my boxers back up in the water."

His words finally registered, and panic surged through her. She always used protection during sex, knew the risks involved. No wonder he'd closed her off, Gabe had probably been in panic mode too. How could they have been so stupid?

She couldn't look at him, and turned instead to glance out over the water.

"Maddie?"

"I heard you." Her voice shook. "I don't really know what to say. Except we screwed up."

He didn't say anything for a moment. "Why don't we get back to the cabin?"

She nodded and stood.

The rest of the hike was again spent in silence, but this time Madison had no desire to break it.

Chapter Thirteen

Gabe volunteered to cook dinner, not ready to take on another one of Madison's adventurous meals. She lay down on the couch in the living room, saying she wanted to try to get a nap in.

He watched her over the counter in the kitchen as he threw something together for them to eat. She seemed tired and stressed. *And it's all my damned fault.*

She shouldn't have to worry about this, too. The unprotected sex slip up. Not with everything else on her mind. Playing out his sexual fantasy on the lake hadn't been an impulse move. He'd planned the whole thing. He'd even remembered to secure a condom in the waistband of his boxers. Things had just happened so fast, had gotten so hot and so out of control.

Damn. What if she got pregnant? The thought had gone through his head only about two hundred times in the last couple of hours. He knew what he would do, what his aunt would have wanted him to do. So why didn't the idea horrify him more?

"You're thinking about it again, aren't you?"

Gabe just about dropped the pot of spaghetti he was in the process of draining and glanced back at her.

"Yeah. Are you?"

"Yes."

She didn't sit up, so he couldn't see her face.

Her voice sounded flat when she went on, "I just want you to know that I'm clean. I was tested about a month ago for everything during a routine physical. You don't have to worry about that part."

"Same on my end," he replied. "But that's not what's really worrying me. Are you on birth control?"

"No," she replied after a moment. "I stopped taking the Pill because Bradley and I stopped having sex."

The thought of her ex touching her sent a burning stab of jealousy through him. He ignored it. *Focus on the present, Gabe, not her past lovers.*

"So there's a chance you could get pregnant." It wasn't a question.

"A little one. But I doubt it," she said hesitantly. "I've never been all that regular with my periods. I should be okay..."

"But we won't know until you get it, or you take a test in a few weeks," he finished for her.

"I guess so."

"Maybe we should talk about the *what if* factor—"

"We're blowing this out of proportion, Gabe." She stood and walked over to him, placing her hand over his. "Let's wait until we know for sure. There's no sense in freaking out this soon."

He hesitated and then nodded. "You're right. I'm just usually a lot more careful and it's pissing me off that I slipped. I'm sorry, Maddie."

His words reminded Madison of his casualness with women. Before, it had never bothered her, had even made him the perfect man to have rebound sex with. But this time it got to her, made her the slightest bit jealous. Scratch that, a lot jealous. *You have no right to jealousy.*

Gabe went back into the kitchen, but she could tell he still had thoughts about the pregnancy thing.

"Dinner will be ready in a minute."

"I'm not all that hungry." And she wasn't. The thought of food made her stomach twist. "I think I'm going to go take that bath now."

"You didn't eat lunch, either," he pointed out with a frown.

Madison shrugged as she walked toward the bathroom. Trying to placate him, she said, "If you leave me a plate, I'll heat some up later."

He looked like he wanted to argue, but then nodded. "Let me know if you need anything."

"I will. Thanks."

After locking the bathroom door, Madison turned on the faucets and began to fill the tub. Her hands shook as she tested the water temperature.

What if she *were* pregnant?

Madison started stripping off her clothes and sighed. She shook her head and climbed into the tub. God, they'd sure been stupid.

And things had been going so great between them. What had started as a rebound was turning into something more.

She grabbed a wrapped bar of soap on the side of the tub and pulled off the paper.

Denying things had changed between her and Gabe had become useless at this point. Her first clue had been the butterflies in her stomach, a sensation she'd assumed would go away after they had sex the first time. It hadn't. It'd only seemed to intensify. All he had to do was smile and she got all atwitter.

And with each layer Gabe revealed about himself, the more of him there was to like, from his secret talent as a photographer to his surprisingly good meals. What would she discover next? That he was great with kids?

Kids...babies. Madison ran the soap over her body and groaned in frustration. Yeah, maybe things had been changing between her and Gabe. The key word being had. But there was nothing like a pregnancy scare to screw up a potential relationship.

Gabe woke first the next morning and glanced down at Madison, who still slept. Although they'd slept next to one another that night, he felt like, emotionally, they were miles apart.

Damn. He touched her cheek with regret. If only he could take away the awkwardness that had sprouted up between them. There were dark circles under her eyes, which wasn't a surprise since she'd tossed and turned all night.

He got out of the bed and reached for his pants. He had to put the condom slip-up out of his mind. Obsessing over it wouldn't change anything and would only make things more difficult between them.

"What time is it?" Madison asked in a drowsy voice.

He zipped up his jeans and turned to face her. "Almost eight-thirty. You can go back to sleep if you want. Sundays are good for having a lazy morning."

"Is it only Sunday?" She sat up and yawned. "I feel like the robbery happened a month ago, but it was just on Wednesday."

He nodded. So much had happened since then. In five days they'd gone from having separate lives to being lovers who were living together.

"I'll just get up." Madison climbed out of bed after him. "I can't sleep."

Guilt stabbed at his gut again, but he pushed it aside and went with his decision to look forward and not back.

"I was about to head into town and hit the grocery store." His mouth twitched. "There's even an espresso stand on the way."

"Oh! There is a God!" She moaned and ran to her suitcase. "Give me five minutes."

As they drove into town, Madison stared out the window at the passing scenery. She smiled, a sense of calm overwhelming her. Maybe it was the enchantment of the beauty of it all, trees and untouched land everywhere.

"This island is beautiful. It's so untainted."

"Well, somewhat." Gabe glanced at her. "Once you head up north, you reach the navy base and every fast food chain imaginable."

"Ooo." Her eyes lit up. "You know that sounds pretty good. I could go for a cheeseburger—"

"I'll make you one," he promised. "This island is too long to go in search of the nearest McDonald's. Besides, burgers on the barbeque taste ten times better."

"We're going to barbeque burgers when we get back?" She clapped her hands. "How fun! We have to get onions and pickles."

"And breath mints as well, apparently," he teased.

She laughed and looked out the window. What a relief that the tension from yesterday had faded. They were back to the flirting and having fun. The mistake probably still lingered in his mind, but maybe he'd done the same thing she had—decided to not think about it for now.

Gabe turned the car off of the main highway, and she returned her gaze to the road ahead. She could see the grocery store in the distance, with the tiny wooden drive-through espresso stand.

"Oooh..." Madison sighed. She could already taste the fluffy foam of a latté with the strong bite of coffee under it.

Gabe laughed. "You sound like you're having an orgasm."

"It may be better than one."

"Sounds like a challenge." He grinned as he pulled up to the window.

"Hi, folks," the teenaged girl inside chirped with a bright smile. "What can I get you?"

"I'll have a tall, sugar-free vanilla, nonfat latté," Madison said and glanced at Gabe.

He hesitated. "Are you sure you don't want a decaf?"

"Decaf? That's sacrilegious." She scowled and her eyes went wide as she realized his thoughts had turned to the pregnancy scare. "Gabe! For the love of—"

"Okay, okay." He raised his hands in surrender to halt her sharp response.

"And what about you? Can I get you something, sir?" the girl asked with a curious smile.

"Me, oh. Yeah..." He shrugged and looked over the menu. "If you could just give me a large cup of milk, that'd be great."

"You just want milk?" Madison and the girl asked at the same time.

"Yeah," he smiled apologetically. "I'm just not a coffee guy. Remember, Maddie?"

"Nothing in it then," the girl repeated. "That's fine, I get that every now and then. Did you want nonfat or two percent?"

"Two percent."

"All right, I'll have those for you guys in just a few minutes."

The girl went to make their drinks and Maddie watched her walk away with a thoughtful expression.

"Why is it, nowadays, that it's almost required for a coffee stand to hire attractive young women in low-cut tops? Have you noticed that?"

"I've only noticed one hot woman." He reached out to trace her mouth. "But she owns her own shop and wears some form-hiding apron instead of a low-cut top."

"Hmm." Madison grinned. "So you think if I showed some cleavage, my sales would go up?"

"Maybe the apron isn't all that bad."

"Cute." She nudged him. "So you like just plain milk, huh?"

"Milk does a body good."

"So they say. You must drink a ton of the stuff." She ran an amused glance down his body.

When her gaze made the return trip to his face, their eyes locked. Her expression softened, and in the silence, they managed to communicate the needed apologies from yesterday.

He reached out and took her hand, giving it a gentle squeeze. Madison smiled at him and squeezed back.

"All right." The girl returned to the window, holding out the two drinks. "That'll be five dollars even."

Gabe released her hand to take out his wallet. He handed the girl eight dollars and took the drinks from her.

"Thanks." The girl's smile widened at the tip. "You folks

have a great day."

Madison gave Gabe a considering look as he drove away, sipping on his milk. He was a great tipper too. That was the next layer.

"How's your drink?" Gabe nodded toward her cup.

Madison glanced down, having forgotten she was even holding it.

"Oh, let me try it." She took a sip and gave a small shrug. "It's pretty good."

"Not as good as Sarah's, I'll bet."

"Nobody's are as good as Sarah's," Madison replied, and frowned. During the past couple of days, she'd forgotten she was out a barista.

She hated to lose Sarah. Lord, she hoped they'd catch the Bandit soon. Hiring someone else was going to be a real pain.

"You're scowling. What brought that on?"

She shook her head. "Oh, that's right, you don't know. Sarah quit. She's too afraid to work for me anymore."

"Makes sense," Gabe agreed. "Why put yourself in that kind of danger if you don't have to?"

"Hello—I'd like to be able to stay in business here." She rolled her eyes. "If you keep supporting my lack of employees, my shop's going to sink like the Titanic."

"Don't think of it like that." He steered the car into a spot at the grocery store. "Think of it like you're delaying your opening. When we catch the Bandit, you can reopen the shop and start making money again."

She took another sip of coffee. "But in the meantime, I'm still making payments on the equipment and paying rent on the shop space."

"We'll have him within a week." Gabe looked over and

caught her gaze. "I know it, Maddie. This guy is not getting away. Are you struggling to make the payments?"

"No," she admitted. "I have money put aside. I didn't know how business would be initially."

"See, you'll be fine." He touched her hand. "Are you ready to go get those groceries?"

Madison's stomach rumbled. "You'd better believe it. I'm looking forward to that barbeque now."

Chapter Fourteen

After they got back to the cabin, Gabe deposited the three sacks of groceries onto the counter.

"Hey, do you mind unloading these while I check my email real quick?"

"No problem," Madison replied, already reaching into the first bag and pulling out the ground beef. She felt so domestic, like the little housewife or something. It was rare that she went grocery shopping. Eating out was just so much easier. "Are you expecting something important?"

He booted up his laptop and glanced over at her. "I gave Brian—you know, my partner, the guy who was watching you on Friday—my email address in case they have any news."

"Oh, right. Hey, if he wrote you, ask him how dinner with Sarah went."

"Ah, that's right, they were going to go on a date."

"I know—it's so cute." She put away the gallon of milk; they'd had to compromise on one percent seeing as he declared himself a stout two percent guy and she survived on nonfat. "Did he write?"

"Doesn't look like it," Gabe replied. "Your brother did, though. Hold on while I read it."

"Cool, let me know what he says." She folded the empty

paper sacks and placed them under the sink.

With nothing left to do, she grabbed an apple and went to sit on the couch next to Gabe.

"Well, damn."

"What's up?"

He set the laptop down on the coffee table and sighed, turning to look at her.

"Eric and Lannie moved up the wedding date."

"Up? Are you serious? It was already a fast wedding. How up are we talking? And why?" She bit into the apple and held it up to him, offering a bite.

He shook his head. "Next month. Eric got word that he has to go to Cuba in June for three months."

"No, really? Poor Eric. And they'd rather bump it up than hold off?" Madison took another bite of her apple. "I'll bet Lannie's pissed."

"He didn't say." Gabe scrolled down the email. "But they want us to meet them in Seattle to talk about some wedding stuff tomorrow night."

"Oh." She frowned. "We can't do that, can we? We'd risk blowing our cover, so to speak."

Gabe grew quiet for a moment. "There may be a way to pull it off. We're not going to your shop or apartment, or even my place. As long as we're smart about it, we could probably do this. We can catch a boat an hour or two before dinner and meet up with them, then head back afterwards."

"Are you sure? If you'd rather we skip it, I'm okay. I'm sure they'd understand if we told them we couldn't make it."

"I'm sure. In fact, I'm certain this was all Lannie's idea, because Eric would never ask us to come if he knew it risked your safety." He smiled at her. "But I think a little night out

159

would be a good break for us. Besides, I'm sure you're getting bored up here."

"Are you kidding?" Madison sighed. "It's been amazing. I love it here, it's so relaxing."

"I'm glad." He leaned forward and kissed her cheek. "I'm going to go start the barbeque."

She watched him disappear out onto the back porch and glanced at the open laptop. So what else did her brother have to say in the email? Did he suspect anything was going on between her and Gabe?

Biting her lip, she leaned forward and started reading the email. Yes, a slight invasion of privacy, but he'd just left it sitting there. She was halfway through reading it when her brows drew together in a scowl.

Besides all the details on the dinner, Eric had also wanted to warn Gabe about Lannie's newest idea. An idea that involved setting him up with her maid of honor.

How ridiculous! Madison hurried and stood, not wanting Gabe to catch her reading his email. She shouldn't have even read it in the first place. Now, she was just annoyed. But it wasn't like she'd expected to find anything like that in Eric's letter.

"How do you want it?" Gabe asked, coming back into the house.

"What?" She gave him a sharp look.

"Your burger. Rare, medium, well-done, on fire..."

"Well-done."

Gabe reached into the fridge to pull out the ground beef.

"This'll be the best burger you've ever had," he promised, his grin pure arrogance.

"I've had some good burgers," she warned, pushing aside

the jealousy that had flared a moment ago. Gabe was with her for now, and she'd just have to remember that.

On his way back out to the porch, he paused to kiss her on the lips.

"If I'm lying, I'll make it up to you later. Any way you want me to, *mi vida*."

Madison raised an eyebrow. "Now I'm almost hoping it'll be bad."

He laughed and went back outside.

§

Monday afternoon they were off the island and driving south on the freeway, heading out to meet Eric and Lannie.

Gabe looked over at Maddie, who'd drifted in and out of sleep during the drive over. They'd stayed awake having sex half the night, this time taking the necessary precautions. And even though she'd declared the burger the best she'd ever eaten, he'd still spent part of the night with his mouth between her legs. He loved the taste of her, the feel of her. She'd become his vice.

"Aren't we running a little early?" she asked, yawning. "I thought dinner wasn't until six."

"It isn't." He looked at her again. "I thought we'd go down to Pike Place Market and walk around, maybe pick up some fresh fruit and homemade bread for breakfast."

"Oh, yum. Great idea, Gabe."

She sat up and glanced outside the window; they were passing through the tall buildings of downtown and making their way toward the waterfront.

"I haven't been down there in a few years."

"Me either." He found a parking garage a few blocks from the market and parked. "Let's head out."

A half-hour later they maneuvered through the crowded marketplace, carrying a bag full of fresh strawberries, a loaf of sourdough bread, and a jar of raspberry jam.

"Too bad we're not going straight home," he commented as they stopped at the fish market to watch the workers tossing fresh salmon to each other. "I'd love to pick up some of that."

"I don't know. I like salmon when it comes to me prepared on a plate. But when I have to see it flying through the air," she wrinkled her nose, "and smell that really fishy smell, well, I get a little grossed out."

Gabe laughed and shook his head. Why wasn't he surprised?

"Maybe when we get back into town for good, we can throw a barbeque and get some. I'll prepare it and you never have to see or smell a thing."

"That sounds wonderful." She glanced up at him and smiled. "You spoil me."

Interesting. He'd made a comment on their future together, sort of, and she hadn't even flinched. In fact, she'd seemed excited by the prospect. Maybe this meant she had started to view things between them differently, as more than just a rebound. The idea settled better with him than he expected.

"We should head out and meet up with your brother."

Madison glanced at her watch and nodded. "You're right, especially with rush-hour traffic."

They backtracked through the market and it wasn't until they'd emerged onto the street that they spoke again.

"I was thinking..." Maddie bit her lip. "When we meet up with everyone we should just try to keep things between us quiet. Make sure nobody suspects we're going at it like rabbits."

Gabe flinched internally, but outwardly he managed a casual shrug for her benefit. "No problem. I'm not much in the mood to get decked by your brother tonight."

She gave him a sharp look and then a hesitant smile. "Great, I'm glad we're on the same wavelength here. It's just that it's none of their business that we're having sex. So if we could make it look like you don't even know that I exist...you know, just like it was a few years ago."

"Say no more." And he meant it. His jaw hardened.

He might as well have been her pool boy. Fine to go to bed with, but she'd never acknowledge it had happened. God, it was irritating how easily she could just turn it on and off. She was a damned faucet. It wasn't that easy for him. His emotions, usually kept in check, weren't so easy to dismiss this time.

And now she wanted him to sit through a dinner and pretend that she wasn't in his every thought. Act like she didn't exist. Right. It was as simple as that. Bullshit.

Might as well get started right away. He let go of her hand and increased his pace to the parking garage.

Madison tuned out the bad traffic while Gabe drove to the restaurant where they were meeting for dinner. Irritation had been eating at her for a while now and she didn't have much trouble pinpointing why. When throwing out the suggestion for them to keep things quiet, she'd been testing the waters, not certain what to expect—maybe for him to argue against it, or perhaps agree after extended persuading.

She certainly hadn't expected the immediate agreement and the joke about her brother getting pissed. Or the way he'd just dropped her hand in the street, like he couldn't wait to get started with the charade.

Shelli Stevens

She fiddled with a strand of hair. *You brought this on, Madison, don't jump down his throat.* Besides, it was for the best. It would just complicate things if word got out that they were lovers. Eric wouldn't be thrilled.

And this dinner was about Eric and Lannie, not Gabe and her.

Still, her mouth tightened. She didn't like the way they'd left things.

Ten minutes later they were parked and walking into a vacant elevator that went up to the restaurant. Gabe pushed the button to their floor, and the moment the doors closed, Maddie grabbed him.

"We've got a few more seconds," she muttered before she dragged his mouth down onto hers.

He didn't try to stop her, but delved his tongue into her mouth. Madison sucked on his tongue, digging her nails into his shoulders. She moaned as he ran his hands down her back to squeeze her ass, tilting her head to give him deeper access to her mouth.

When the elevator dinged, signaling that they'd reached their floor, they stumbled apart and went to opposite sides of the elevator. Madison wiped her mouth, as if she could diminish the swollenness of her lips.

"You've got some lipstick." She gestured toward him.

Gabe rubbed the back of his hand across his mouth to clear any physical evidence she'd left behind.

When the doors slid open, he waited for her to step out and then followed behind her.

Chapter Fifteen

Madison took a steadying breath, trying to appear calm as she approached the hostess and gave her Eric's name. A moment later they followed the woman through the restaurant.

She spotted her brother at the back of the restaurant. Lannie sat beside him, her head tilted toward his in an intimate way as she whispered something to him.

Eric must have noticed their approach, because he looked their way and gave a broad grin.

"You guys made it." Lannie gestured for them to sit. "I'm glad to see you're both okay. You had us worried."

Eric stood and clapped Gabe on the back in greeting. "Glad you're all right, man. It looks like you're doing a good job keeping Madison safe."

"Hey, you know I keep my promises," Gabe replied and sat at the circular table next to Eric.

Madison sat next to Lannie, putting a bit of space between her and Gabe.

"They gave us a big table," she commented, looking around with a bright smile.

"Oh, yes, well Christina's coming, too." Lannie glanced off toward the reception area. "She should be here any moment."

"Christina?" Madison reached for the water glass in front of her.

"My maid of honor."

Damn! Madison forced a smile.

"Ah." Gabe sighed and she caught the knowing look that passed between Eric and him. She took a drink of the water and willed herself not to get pissed off.

Eric's email had warned Gabe about the maid of honor, but Madison hadn't expected her to show up tonight.

"I didn't realize you were inviting the whole wedding party." Madison forced a smile. "So there's more coming?"

"No." Lannie glanced back at her. "Well, we really just needed to go over some things with the best man and maid of honor, so it'll just be the five of us."

They didn't even need her here. She forced an answering smile. "I kinda feel like the fifth wheel. Are you sure you want me here?"

"Of course we want you here," Lannie insisted with a frown. "We want your input. And we haven't seen you since Gabe whisked you off to God knows where. We're going to be family soon, Madison!"

Taking another sip of water saved her from having to respond. She liked Lannie, really she did. But, even though the woman's intentions were good, setting Gabe up with someone else was the quickest way to piss her off.

But Lannie didn't know that, and wouldn't know that unless she said something. And that wouldn't be happening anytime soon.

"There's Christy now."

Madison glanced up at Lannie's exclamation, seeking out her new and unwanted nemesis. The woman making her way across the restaurant was petite and blonde, with sparkling blue eyes.

"I'm glad you could make it," Lannie said when she'd reached the table. "This is Madison, Eric's sister. And this is Gabe, Eric's best friend and the best man. In other words, your date down the aisle!"

Subtle, Lannie. Real subtle. Madison kept a polite smile pasted on her face.

Christy sat between Madison and Gabe and gave them each a bright smile.

"I'm glad I finally get to meet you both. I've heard so much about you two."

Madison didn't miss the way the woman's gaze lingered on Gabe for a moment longer than necessary.

She snapped open her menu and stared at the entrees in front of her, not bothering to try to read them, just trying to hide the scowl on her face.

Lannie cleared her throat. "Gabe, Christy teaches Spanish at Westwood High School, and in the summer is a salsa dancing instructor."

"Really?" Gabe replied and asked Christy a question in Spanish.

Madison's jaw clenched as the other woman replied and giggled in a way that was just as cute as she was. She didn't understand a word they had said. She'd taken French in high school, and even that hadn't been her best subject.

"I haven't been here in a while," Madison interrupted, glancing around the table. "Does anyone know what's good?"

"Oh." Christy blinked and then shrugged. "I've never been here before. I have to confess I don't eat dinner out much. Like Lannie told you, I'm a teacher and, on my salary, I try to save money." She laughed. "But you know what? I love to cook, so it works out well."

Great, she was a petite and pretty Betty Crocker. Madison glanced at Gabe. Probably exactly his type. He did look impressed, but at least he didn't appear to be at the salivating stage yet.

She turned her gaze back to Christy and looked her over again. Funny that she'd claimed to be a poor teacher, because Madison would have bet anything that the dress she wore wasn't cheap.

"That's a great dress, Christy. Where did you get it?"

"Thanks." Christy glanced down at the summery floral dress and smiled. "Believe it or not, I got it at a thrift shop. I confess—I'm addicted to second-hand shops and online auctions."

"Doesn't it just make you jealous?" Lannie asked with a sigh. "I go into a thrift shop and can't find a thing. Christy goes in and comes out with Ralph Lauren."

The rest of the table shared a laugh while Madison's stomach churned with jealousy.

"What do you do, Madison?" Christy turned to face her with a curious look.

"I own an espresso shop in Seattle."

"Wow, hats off to you. I couldn't get through my ninth graders without coffee. I'll have to stop by some time. What's the name of your shop?"

"Ooo La Latté."

"Nice, very original. Although I'm not sure I've heard of it." Her perfect eyebrows curved downwards into a puzzled frown.

"I just opened last week," Madison admitted. "And got robbed three days later. Gabe made me shut down until we catch the guy."

Christy's mouth gaped and she glanced to Lannie and Eric as if for confirmation.

"It's true." Eric nodded. "I've been out of my mind worrying about her."

"But you don't need to be." Madison's smile felt a little more genuine this time. "I've been with Gabe twenty-four hours a day. And I have to say, he does his job very well." She couldn't resist adding, "I'm very pleased with our...arrangement."

Christy's look of surprise was priceless, and her demeanor was a little more hesitant when she glanced back at Gabe. *That's right,* Madison told her silently, *there may be no signs up, but you're poaching on someone else's territory.*

"Gabe's a police officer," Lannie hurried to explain. "Eric wanted the best protection for Madison and Gabe fits the bill. She's almost like a little sister to him. Right, Gabe?"

Gabe looked at Madison and raised an eyebrow. She knew what he was thinking—that she'd made the rules and he was just following them. But she swore he enjoyed this.

"Right, Lannie." He picked up his water glass. "Maddie's just like a sister."

Madison looked away. God, she wished he were sitting across from her so she could kick him.

Eric looked from Gabe to Madison to Lannie, and then shook his head. Obviously this wasn't a discussion he planned on wading into anytime soon.

"Who's up for champagne?" he asked instead.

Madison and Gabe declined, while everyone else seemed delighted by the idea. The focus turned toward what to order for dinner and conversation died while they all scanned their menus.

The waitress came and took their orders, then left, leaving

them with a basket of bread and some chunky tomato spread to put on it.

Eric took the basket and offered a piece to Lannie, who shook her head.

"No, sweetie. You know I'm going low-carb 'til the wedding."

Madison resisted the urge to roll her eyes and reached for the basket. Lannie already looked to be about a size two; the poor woman would disappear if she lost too much weight. Eric seemed to share her thoughts, but didn't comment.

Lannie folded her hands on the table and leaned forward to face the rest of them.

"So, the first thing we need to discuss is bridesmaid dresses and the men's tuxes."

"Oh, yes! So what are you thinking?" Christy giggled. "This is so much fun."

Madison bit back a groan. Yeah, like scrubbing floors. It was going to be a long night. She sighed and grabbed a second piece of bread.

By the time their dinner arrived, Madison didn't want to hear another word about fabrics, colors, or styles. Most of the time she loved exploring the world of fashion, but there was something about squeezing fashion into that tiny bridesmaid category that took all the fun out of it. Not to mention trying to make multiple women look good in the same dress. Talk about a mission impossible.

She stabbed a piece of lettuce from her Greek salad and glanced over at the men. They'd been deep in discussion about the status of the Mariners for the last half-hour. Gabe said something to Eric, but his gaze drifted over to her and his lips curved into a half-smile. Her lips flattened into a tight smile in response and she continued eating her salad.

"Gabe, yours looks amazing." Christy nodded toward Gabe's plate, even as she twirled her fork around a fettuccine noodle on her own. "Is it as good as it looks?"

Madison's attention snapped to the pair; she'd have to be deaf and stupid to miss the suggestive tone in the other woman's voice.

"It's not bad," he agreed, without responding to her not-so-subtle attempts at flirting.

Good boy—don't lead her on.

"Did you want to try some?"

What? Madison's jaw clenched. What was he doing?

Christy laughed. "If you're sure you don't mind."

Madison watched as Gabe cut a piece of his chicken and lifted it onto her plate. Christy ate it and gave a sigh that should have been saved for the bedroom.

"Wow, that's just sinful." She wound her fork around a length of fettuccine and stabbed a shrimp. "Now you try mine."

Gabe held out his plate, but she ignored it and raised the fork to his mouth.

Madison's eyes widened. *If you eat that, you aren't getting laid tonight.* He didn't even hesitate or look her way, just opened his mouth and accepted what Christy offered him. Madison's blood pressure shot up, though she refused to reveal any outward reaction.

Lannie seemed delighted with the display, and nudged Eric with a grin. He gave her a brief smile, and his gaze lifted to connect with Madison's. Something in the look he gave her made her wonder for a moment if her brother suspected what was going on between her and Gabe.

She dropped her gaze and tossed her napkin on the table, standing. "I'll be back in a moment. I'm going to run to the restroom."

She escaped the table in as casual and dignified a manner as she could manage. If she had to watch Christy's blatant flirting for one more moment, she was going to hurl into her salad.

The bathroom appeared blessedly empty as she stood in front of the mirror, scowling at her reflection. Gabe had gotten her so hyped about the natural look the other day that she'd forgone makeup tonight. And instead of dressing to the max, which was her normal routine for going to a nice restaurant, she'd worn khakis and a sweater set.

Had she known Señorita Christy would be joining them, looking like a petite supermodel and flirting like her life depended on it, Madison would have tried a little harder.

The soft swish of the bathroom door swinging open had her raising her gaze to see who had come in.

Now why wasn't she surprised to see the object of her annoyance walking toward her?

Chapter Sixteen

"Hi, Madison." Christy gave her a bright smile.

"Hello." Madison turned on the sink to wash her hands. She expected the other woman to disappear into a stall, but instead she leaned against the sink and watched her.

"What's going on?" she asked when Christy still didn't say anything.

Christy fidgeted with a ring on her right hand and offered a tentative shrug. "I was hoping to get the chance to speak to you alone."

"Speak to me about...?"

"Gabe."

Of course. "What about Gabe?"

"Lannie told me he was available," she went on. "And said that she thought we would hit it off."

"Oh, yeah?" Madison laughed, hoping it didn't sound as forced as it felt. *For the love of God, somebody shoot me now!* "Lannie's quite the matchmaker."

"No kidding." Christy seemed to relax a bit as her smile widened. "I think Gabe is pretty hot and he seems like an intriguing guy. You know, he has that whole dark and dangerous vibe."

Yes, she was very familiar with that vibe. Madison looked

toward the door, wanting to get the hell out of this room and away from this woman. Having a root canal would have been preferable to continuing this conversation.

"I hadn't noticed." She deliberately kept her tone bland.

"Oh?" Christy raised an eyebrow. "Well, that's what I wanted to ask you, Madison—if there is something going on with you and Gabe in a romantic sense. I'm not one to step on any toes..." She trailed off.

I have the perfect opportunity. I could tell Christy to back off, and that Gabe and I are a couple.

But technically they weren't. So as much as she wanted to, she couldn't say that to Christy. Not to mention if she admitted she was sleeping with Gabe, Lannie would know about it before the night was over. And if Lannie knew about it, then Eric would know about it. That's when things would really get sticky.

Eric wouldn't be too pleased knowing that she was sleeping with his best friend. The reputation that had made Gabe a perfect candidate for a rebound would be the reason Eric would flip out if he knew about it. Besides, what right did she have to lay claim to Gabe, anyway? If she were honest with herself, she had none.

"Gabe is a family friend," Madison heard herself say. "There's no romance between us."

Just sex. Maybe more, but neither of them was ready to acknowledge it.

"A friend," Christy repeated with a nod. "Wonderful. Well, then, I think I'll go back and see if I can make any more progress with that fascinating man. Wish me luck."

"Good luck." The two words had her stomach clenching.

She watched Christy disappear out of the restroom and

wished she could hate her. Unfortunately, besides the somewhat annoying perkiness, the woman seemed overall a likeable person. If the circumstances had been different, Madison would have declared it an instant friendship.

Instead, she sat here hoping Gabe didn't bail on her to get involved with the cute schoolteacher. She pushed a hand wearily through her hair.

When she came back to the table, Christy had moved full-throttle into flirting. Gabe smiled at whatever she said, and glanced up as Madison approached the table.

She averted her gaze, not wanting him to see any emotions that she might not yet have under control.

"We're looking over the dessert menu, Madison." Eric passed her one. "What do you want?"

Madison looked down at the menu. It all looked unappealing to her right now.

"I think I overdid it on bread," she replied. "Thanks, but I'll pass."

"Oh, good." Lannie grinned and patted her hand. "I hate being the lone one to forego the sugar. I can't wait until I'm married and I can eat all unhealthy again."

The waiter reappeared to take their order. After Eric had ordered a simple bowl of ice cream, the waiter turned to Christy.

"We're going to share the tiramisu." She gestured toward Gabe.

Madison's stomach knotted further and a bitter taste filled her mouth.

The waiter nodded. "Would you like an extra plate with that?"

"No, that's all right." She looked at Gabe and her smile

widened.

"Maybe an extra fork," Gabe inserted.

Well, at least he'd asked for an extra fork. Why had she imagined that Gabe would actually discourage Christy's flirting? She knew his track record. Gabe went through women like she went through shoes. Madison glanced at the watch on her wrist. How much longer did she have to put up with this?

Though she tried not to watch while the two ate off the same plate, her gaze drifted over of its own accord.

The lousy piece of crap. Her hands clenched under the table as she vowed that there was no way she would stay another day on the island with him. He could come back to Seattle and bring Christy back to his house for some real education. She didn't give a damn so long as she didn't have to watch it.

"I've got it, Gabe," Eric said. "I'm paying for everyone's dinner."

Madison looked up to see that the dessert plates had been cleared and Gabe and her brother were arguing over the bill.

"Better let him get it, Gabe." She gave a brief smile. "After all, like teachers, cops don't make that much money."

Her cheeks burned with shame. Oh, Lord, why had she said that? Why? How utterly bitchy of her. Everyone's blunt stares seemed to agree with her inner consensus.

"And I suppose the espresso business does so much better," Gabe replied, his tone soft and cold.

He wanted to fight? Well bring it on. "Well, gee." She sighed. "I'm sure it would, if you'd let me open my shop for business."

"Madison?" Eric gave her a reproachful glance. "Why are you coming down so hard on Gabe? He's doing me a favor by watching over you. Any advice or decisions he's making are for your own safety."

Of course, she seethed. How could she have forgotten she was a favor for Eric? This was so unlike her, though. It was rare that she let her emotions get this out of hand, and never was she so foolish as to let anyone see when it happened. She took a deep breath, willing herself to calm down.

"You're right, Eric," she forced herself to say in an agreeable tone. "I don't know what came over me. I'm getting a bit of a migraine, and it makes me short-tempered."

"Then we should head out," Gabe insisted, standing. "We have a long drive ahead of us."

Madison wanted to tell him she would just stay here, but all her luggage was up on Whidbey. She rose from her seat and grabbed her purse. "Thank you for dinner, Eric."

"Don't forget the rehearsal dinner is in two weeks," Lannie mentioned quickly. "I hope you feel better, Madison."

Eric leaned forward to shake hands with Gabe.

"Thanks for everything, Gabe." He'd spoken the words low, but Madison could still hear him. "I'm sure she didn't mean it— she must be having a bad day."

Gabe said something in response, but this time she couldn't hear.

Christy looked flustered as she watched them get ready to leave. She touched Gabe's jacket and leaned forward to whisper something into his ear. She wasn't quite as inconspicuous when she slipped him a scrap of paper.

Ugh! Having seen enough, Madison turned on her heel and walked away from the restaurant to the elevator. She jammed the button for the parking garage, hoping that she'd left quickly enough that she wouldn't have to share the elevator with Gabe.

But luck wasn't on her side. He walked up and stood next to her.

"Did you have a nice dinner, Maddie?"

Her jaw clenched. "Lovely. And you?"

"It was very nice."

The doors to the elevator slid open and they both stepped inside, waiting quietly for a moment.

The doors slid shut and the pleasantries disappeared.

"Are you going to explain your temper tantrum back at the table?" Gabe turned to look at her with cold eyes.

"I have a headache." Madison looked away, completely in control of her emotions again.

"Right, the headache excuse," he replied with a slight edge. "You seem like the type to use it."

Her teeth snapped together, the control slipping, but she forced her lips into a smile. "What can I say? It can be very useful."

"Ah...maybe that's why Bradley dumped you."

"Oh, you did not just say that." Madison's head whipped around to face him, but he had already stridden through the doors that had just opened.

She reached the car a moment after him and climbed into the passenger seat, belting herself in with more force than necessary. The control she'd regained disappeared once again.

"Don't presume that you know me or anything about me." Her blood boiled, and it was a miracle her voice didn't shake since her hands were so badly.

"I wouldn't have to presume if you'd just calm down and talk to me about it." He turned to glare at her. "I want to know why you freaked out at dinner."

"I didn't freak out," she snapped. "I was just fine, considering I had to watch you mentally undress Christy all night."

Damn! That thought wasn't supposed to have left her head. Madison closed her eyes and didn't bother looking at Gabe. It was just what he'd wanted her to say and they both knew it.

"You're the one who made the rules tonight, Maddie." All of a sudden he sounded weary. "You told me to act like you didn't exist. What was I supposed to do? Eric knows me inside and out. He knows that I wouldn't brush off such blatant flirting."

"You didn't have to flirt back."

"Didn't I?" He glanced at her. "Didn't I, Maddie? Be honest with yourself for once. If I hadn't flirted back, Eric would have known something was up. Would you have been prepared to deal with his suspicions?"

Be honest with yourself. Her stomach twisted. "No. I wouldn't have wanted to deal with that." She took a deep breath. "I don't want to draw attention to what we've got going on between us. That's personal."

He nodded. "Understandable."

She looked away and said in a quiet voice, "But I didn't like seeing you getting pawed by some other woman, either."

He stayed silent for a moment. His hand covered hers and she jumped, startled at the contact. Her gaze crept over to look at him.

He watched her with a gentle expression. "Did it kill you to admit that?"

"Just about," she whispered. But it was also a relief to have admitted it. It was so tiring trying to pretend he didn't affect her, that she didn't mind if he flirted with other women.

Her shoulders crumpled and she shook her head. "I'm

sorry, Gabe. I'm behaving like a spoiled kid."

His hand squeezed hers. "Well, I'm sorry I hurt you. And I want you to know I'm not interested in Christy in the slightest."

Madison glanced down at their hands, relief flooding through her. "Really? Not even a little? It would be understandable if you were. I mean, she's pretty and sweet. She even speaks Spanish."

"Quit trying to sell me on her attributes or I'm going to think you're her pimp, Maddie," he teased. "I'm not going to deny that she's pretty. But there's just one woman on my mind right now."

"Angelina Jolie?" She grinned, mostly because her stomach turned all fluttery and warm.

"Well, you are both brunettes." They stopped at a traffic light and he leaned over to brush his lips over hers. "But I think you're still in the lead."

Chapter Seventeen

Madison opened her mouth under his, reveling in the invasion of his tongue. The sound of a horn had them pulling apart with reluctance.

Gabe hit the gas and sped through the light just as the skies opened up in a torrent of rain. By the time they reached the ferry, the wind had started and it grew obvious they were in for a storm.

"It's amazing how fast the weather changed," Gabe said once they were parked on the lower level of the ferry. "Do you want to go upstairs?"

She nodded. "I've been in the car for too long. I wouldn't mind getting some air."

They left the car and went upstairs, wandering around the passenger deck before deciding to brave going outside.

Madison winced as the cold rain slapped against her cheeks, but the refreshing air made it worth it.

"You can go inside if you want," she yelled above the wind. "I don't mind staying out here by myself."

"I promised I'd protect you," he called back with a grin and drew her body against him. "Just because it happens to be from the weather makes no difference."

She snuggled into him, feeling safe and warm with her

back pressed against his solid chest. He wrapped the edges of his trench coat around them. It didn't completely encompass her, but it protected her from the brunt of the storm.

They stayed outside the entire ride, with the rain and wind pounding at their faces and a warm heat radiating between their bodies.

When they went back to the car, Madison missed the loss of warmth from Gabe's body, even with the heater on full blast. But the eventual combination of a warm car and the rain outside lulled her into a light sleep.

Gabe glanced over at Madison's sleeping form and a surge of tenderness swelled through him, followed by a growing possessiveness.

He turned his focus back to the road. Tomorrow they should talk. It was time. Despite neither of them having wanted things to get complicated, somewhere along the line they had.

Gabe squinted at the dark road ahead of him. Since it was late and the road was deserted, he flipped on his high-beams. A few seconds later a deer, not even a hundred feet ahead of him, was illuminated in his lights.

He hit the brakes and waited for the deer to move off the road. Madison stirred, but didn't open her eyes.

"Are we there already?" she mumbled.

"Not yet. You can go back to sleep."

"'kay."

A few minutes later she started snoring again as he maneuvered down the wet road.

By the time he pulled up in front of the cabin, the wind had reached its highest peak of the night so far.

Gabe climbed out and ran around to Madison's door,

pulling it open and helping her out as she struggled to wake up.

The trees bent in the wind and the blowing rain hit almost painfully against their skin as they ran inside.

Gabe shut the door behind her and turned to hit the light switch. Nothing happened.

"Did we lose power?" she asked, still groggy.

"Looks like it." He nodded. "I've got a flashlight in my car—I'll be right back."

Madison watched as he disappeared out into the storm, and she glanced into the dark house. She shivered again, but not only because of the cold. Being alone in a cabin without power was kind of creepy. Hell, she'd seen enough horror movies to be scared. She relaxed when he returned a moment later with a flashlight that was three times as big as any she'd ever used.

"That must take a lot of batteries," she said as he flicked it on and shut the front door behind him.

"I rarely use it, so it's all right." He took her hand and led her through the dark room.

Good thing he led, because she couldn't see much. "Should we just call it a night and go to bed?"

"I have a better idea," he suggested. "I was thinking we could pull the blankets off the bed and sleep in the living room. I'll get a fire going in the fireplace."

Warmth flooded through her at his suggestion. How absolutely romantic. "You're right, that is a better idea."

"I thought you'd like it. Sit down for a moment and I'll grab the blankets."

Madison reached down, feeling the couch and sinking onto it. He left her alone again, but she didn't mind as much because she'd already started to visualize the heat of their upcoming fire.

When he returned, he handed her the comforter, a furry blanket, and two pillows.

"All right, I'll leave you these to make our bed on the floor and I'll go get some wood from the shed."

He handed her the flashlight, but she shook her head.

"You're going to need it more than I am, Gabe. It's pitch black out there."

"It's pitch black in here," he pointed out. "And I've been here many times, so I know where I'm going. And there's still a little bit of moonlight."

"All right," she agreed and took the flashlight from him. "Be careful and hurry back."

"Of course." He lowered his head to drop a quick kiss on her mouth. "It's freezing out there."

Once he'd disappeared, Madison pushed aside the coffee table and spread the comforter on the floor. That would have to do for cushioning them. Then she grabbed their pillows and set them down, and afterwards laid the faux fur blanket on top of the comforter.

There. Between the fire and their body heat, that ought to keep them warm.

Gabe reappeared with a stack of logs balanced in his arms and kindling clutched in his fist. Madison rushed forward to help him, relieving him of a couple of logs.

"Thanks." He set the rest down next to the fireplace. "Now all we need is to find some matches."

"Hmm." Madison frowned. "It's times like this I wish I smoked."

Gabe laughed and shook his head. "I think there are some

in the kitchen drawer. Here, I'll take that flashlight back."

Realizing she still had to get ready for bed, she padded off through the darkened cabin.

Lord I'm brave. She felt her way along the wall toward the bathroom. Even though her normal routine for bed took about a half-hour, the fact that she now did it blind made her skip some aspects and pick up the pace. She made her way back to the living room ten minutes later.

"Ah, too bad, she found her nightgown," Gabe commented from his seat next to the small, but steadily growing fire.

"You were hoping I wouldn't?" Madison grinned and sat next to him on the fur blanket.

"Well, I wouldn't have protested nakedness." The fire crackled beside them. "And I have to warn you that I have no intention of going in search of my pajamas."

"Oh, darn. That means I'll be sleeping next to a naked man." She gave a dramatic sigh. "I swear, the sacrifices a girl has to make in a storm."

Gabe laughed softly. "You've got a better sense of humor than I remember, Maddie. Back when you were a teenager..."

"Yes?"

"Well." He shrugged. "You weren't as laid back. You always seemed so focused on being popular and were surrounded by a bunch of uptight snobs."

A prick of guilt stabbed at her stomach. "Yeah..."

Gabe winced. "I'm sorry. I probably shouldn't have said that."

"Don't be sorry. In fact, I agree," she confessed. "I'll be the first to admit that I was a spoiled, materialistic snob back in the day. I think what changed me most was living in Italy. Somehow it put into perspective what I really wanted in life.

That's what made me decide to get my MBA when I got back."

"Italy did all that? Sounds like an impressive place."

"The people were amazing, too. Have you ever been to Europe?"

He shook his head, staring at the fire.

"We should go."

He looked back at her and lifted an eyebrow. "We should go to Europe? Together?"

"I don't know," she replied after a moment. "I was just throwing it out there. I guess I meant you should go. You don't have to go with me, necessarily. I just think you would enjoy it very much."

Gabe scooted closer to her on the blanket, watching the way the fire highlighted the conflicting emotions on her face.

"If you go back, would you go alone?"

"I assume so."

"Aren't there any friends you'd take?"

"I don't have many close friends," she admitted, casting him a sideways glance. "Like I said, I've changed since high school and haven't seen any of those girls in years. And I was so focused in college that I didn't have much time for a social life. The friends I did make are still in Oregon. We call occasionally and email, but you know how it goes."

He kept staring at her with a pensive expression. "I don't have the kind of friendship with them that you have with my brother."

"Most people don't have the kind of friendship that I have with your brother," he acknowledged. "He's like blood."

"Okay, I know you mean that in a good way." She grimaced. "But seeing as we're sleeping together, it makes me really not want to think of you in a brotherly fashion."

186

"Don't worry, there's no danger of that." His lips curved into a half-smile as he touched a strand of her hair. "I stopped thinking of you as a little sister the night of Eric's welcome home party."

"You did?" She sighed and closed her hand around his fingers. "I couldn't tell. You were so hard to read that night. I thought I was losing my touch."

"It took all my will not to bend you over the balcony." He kissed the side of her neck. "And take you right then and there."

"Wow." Madison giggled, heat coursing through her body. "There's a visual. Maybe we should try that the next time you come to dinner at my parents."

"Maybe not." His smile slipped slightly. "I don't think your father would be too happy to know we're sleeping together."

Madison gave a frustrated sigh. "Gabe, you're sleeping with me, not my entire family."

He nodded, but didn't look convinced.

"Has Eric ever said anything to you about keeping away from me?"

"No, Eric's never said a word." He cleared his throat. "But your father has."

Madison frowned and sat up straighter on the blanket. "When? When did he say something? What did he say?"

Gabe shrugged. "He just didn't want you to get hurt again. Told me to be very careful when I was watching over you."

"Was this at lunch last week?"

He nodded.

"Why would he do that?" she asked, shaking her head. "It just doesn't seem like something he'd do. I don't think he was trying to warn you off, necessarily."

"He was worried about your breakup with Bradley," Gabe pointed out. "He thinks you're in a world of hurt."

"Bradley?" Madison snorted. "We'd been on the verge of breaking up since I moved back from Oregon. Even when we lived together, our relationship was dysfunctional."

"You lived together?" Gabe frowned, looking disturbed by the news.

"Yeah." She nudged him in the side and smiled. "Are you jealous?"

He paused. "Yeah, a little."

Her eyes widened, pleasure curling in her belly. "Well, then, I guess we've both had our dose of jealousy for the night."

He didn't reply. What was he thinking about? Had she said the wrong thing?

"How's this rebound thing working out for you, Maddie?"

Rebound? Was she still considering this a rebound relationship? Was he? She looked closely at his face, now really curious as to what he was thinking.

"I think it's going great," she answered carefully. Lord, what should she say? What did he want her to say? "I'm definitely not regretting getting involved with you."

He grunted in response. "So, you think you'll be wrapping up the buffer stage soon?"

"Buffer stage?" Her eyebrows crinkled together. "What are you talking about?"

"You told me I'm the buffer between you and your next relationship," he reminded her. "Do you remember saying that?"

"Oh." She glanced down at her hands. "I guess I did say that."

"I'm just wondering how long you want to keep this up?"

Keep this up? "I don't know. I'm not interested in anyone else right now. I don't see why we can't keep what we've got going."

"Ah, but when you *are* interested in someone else, then that's when our buffer relationship ends?"

Madison gave a short laugh. Was he messing with her head? She sobered when his expression didn't change. *Wow, he was completely serious.*

"Gabe." She hesitated. "I don't understand. Aren't you the guy who doesn't do relationships?"

"I thought I was." He held her gaze. "But I'm not sure of anything anymore. Are you, Maddie?"

It hit her then. So hard that she couldn't speak for a moment. She wasn't sure what she wanted. But she was sure she didn't want to consider Gabe just a fling anymore.

"No. I'm not," she answered in a soft voice. "Maybe we should just see what happens. Not put labels on anything, but just see how it goes."

"As long as we take away the rebound status." Gabe smiled, looking a little more content. "I think it's a little hard on my ego."

Madison laughed and looked straight at him. "Would you answer a question? You can say no. I realize it's personal."

He shrugged. "What do you want to know?"

"Why you became a cop." She hurried on when his expression became shuttered. "I know you've said you don't want to talk about it, but I was hoping you might have changed your mind. That maybe you could trust me—"

"Why?" he interrupted, turning to look in the fire. "Why should you want to know about my past? What difference could it possibly make knowing?"

"I'm not sure it'll make any difference," she admitted, laying a hand on his shoulder. "There's just so much I still don't know about you, things that you've never told me."

His body went rigid, the previous atmosphere of relaxation and flirting gone.

"Well I'm not sure I'm ready to tell all just to appease your curiosity, Maddie."

"It's not just curiosity," she replied in exasperation. "Like you just pointed out, things have changed between us. I care about you. Is that so hard to believe?"

He didn't look away from the fire. "You don't want to care about me. I'm not worth it."

"Gabe." Her heart ached for him. What was hidden behind that wall surrounding his emotions? "Oh, Gabe. Whatever it is, I wish I could take away the pain."

He stayed quiet for a long time. "My pain is nothing compared to what happened to my brother."

Madison blinked at his words. What brother? With caution, she said, "I didn't know you had a brother."

"I don't anymore." Gabe smiled, but it twisted his lips bitterly and lacked warmth. "I killed him."

Chapter Eighteen

He stared at her as if he'd expected her to freak out, maybe shrink back with horror or run from the room terrified. But she didn't believe it, not for moment.

"No, you didn't." She shook her head. "I know you didn't. Tell me the whole story."

"You want the whole story?" Gabe asked, his expression cold. "I had a brother who was six years older than me. His name was Ricardo; everyone called him Ricky. Ricky was amazing. He graduated high school with a 4.0 average and was given a scholarship to UCLA. He never let circumstances like where we lived or who our parents were get in the way of his dreams. He raised me after Mom and Dad died."

Gabe stood, his body rigid as he began to pace in front of the fire.

"He wanted to take me out of the shit-hole neighborhood we were living in." He shrugged. "And I didn't want to go. I didn't see anything wrong with my life. I was a twelve-year-old wannabe gang-banger."

Maddie stayed silent, trying to associate the younger Gabe with the Gabe she knew now. It was impossible and she shook her head.

"Not a pretty little picture, is it?" Gabe asked, misinterpreting her gesture.

"No, I—"

"It gets better," he went on. "When my brother found out I was going to be initiated into a gang, he left school during a final exam. All to come back to stop me from ruining my life."

Madison held her breath.

"My initiation was to beat up an elderly man walking his dog in the park."

"Did you do it?" she asked before she could stop herself. The horrific image flickered through her mind, and nausea raged through her as she waited for his answer.

"I think I would have," Gabe replied. "If Ricky hadn't shown up."

Her relief was immediate, though her instincts deep down told her that he wouldn't have done it.

"No, you wouldn't have. But thank God Ricky was there to stop you."

"Ricky being there was no blessing." Gabe gave a harsh laugh. "It was his death sentence."

Madison's insides twisted and her throat grew tight. She almost didn't want to know, but could guess what happened next.

"There were two of us getting initiated that day. Me and another boy a couple years older than me. His initiation was different." He paused. "He was told to shoot and wound, but not kill, the next person who came down the trail."

She clenched her fists. "Was it Ricky?"

His silence she took as an affirmation. She stood and put a gentle hand on his arm.

"The boy was either a terrible shot or an excellent one." His tone had gone flat, his expression blank. "Because the bullet went straight through Ricky's heart. He died right away."

"You didn't kill him, Gabe."

"I may not have pulled the trigger, but I killed him."

"You were a messed-up kid," she argued. "You were twelve years old, for goodness sake. You were a product of your environment."

"Oh, do you think so?" His tone mocked her now. "So then why wasn't every kid on my block in a gang? Why didn't Ricky join a gang instead of aiming for a college education?"

"You have to stop blaming yourself." She reached up and took his face between both of her hands, forcing him to look at her. "You were a child. Look how far you've come since then."

"But if I hadn't—"

"Ricky chose to come after you. He must have known the risks involved. That showed how much he loved you. And what you've done with your life since shows how much you must have loved him." She met his tormented gaze.

"I'm on the verge of being promoted to head up the gang unit," Gabe admitted, some of the anguish diminishing in his eyes. "It's what I've wanted to do ever since Aunt Martha took me in and helped me get my life in order. If I can make a difference in their lives, just get these kids on track..."

Warmth swept through her. "That's wonderful, Gabe. I really do think it's your calling."

Gabe's hands covered hers and tightened about the wrists.

"Why don't you think I'm a terrible person, Maddie?"

"Because you're not!" she cried. The need to convince him swelled stronger inside her. "God, you're not. You're a wonderful man who had a very difficult upbringing. Please, Gabe, forgive yourself and let it go."

"Maddie." He groaned and pulled her into his arms, his touch gentle as he caressed her cheek. "You should hate me for what I just told you."

"Oh, Gabe. I could never hate you. Never."

He stared down at the woman in his arms. This woman was amazing. She hadn't looked at him with repulsion when he told her about Ricky. The pain in her eyes had been a mirror to his soul. As if they were connected.

He buried his hands in her hair and tilted her head up so he could close his mouth over her parted lips. Madison's eyes drifted shut and she sighed, winding her arms around his neck.

He loved her. God help him, he was in love with Maddie.

Gabe's throat tightened with emotion as he lowered her onto her back on the fur. His mouth urged her lips to part so he could slide his tongue inside. She mimicked the soft and gentle thrusting motion of his tongue as his hand cupped the side of her face.

They made no move to go any further, but continued the slow, sensual kissing.

After a while Madison pulled away and urged him to lie down beside her.

"Let me give you a back rub," she said softly, giving him a glance from under her eyelashes.

A back rub sounded amazing. Gabe didn't argue, just rolled over onto his stomach and folded his arms under his head.

"I'll be right back. I need to grab some lotion." Her feet made little padding sounds across the floor, and she came back and knelt beside him.

"Just relax. Try to focus on the feel of my hands."

"That shouldn't be too hard," he mumbled against his arm.

He heard lotion squirting, and the smell of vanilla reached his nose.

Her soft hands began rubbing the lotion into his naked back. "Your skin is thirsty; it soaked all that lotion up."

He gave a sigh of pleasure when she started to knead him, moving up his shoulders.

She pressed her fingers harder, probed each muscle deeper. His body relaxed under her touch, his eyes drifting shut with drowsiness.

He felt the curtain of her hair tickle his back, and then she dropped a soft kiss on his neck. His body shuddered in response and he started to roll over. "Mmm."

"Not yet, sweetie. I've still got to do your lower back."

"It's not necessary—"

"Nonsense." She gave him a gentle push onto the fur. "Just relax and enjoy."

"Yes, ma'am." He lay back down, smiling as her hand traveled down his waist and further down to his ass.

"I suppose you know how great your butt is," she told him. "It's the best I've ever seen, not to mention felt."

Amusement pricked through him. "Like it that much, do you?" He flexed the muscles in his buttocks so the flesh contracted under her fingers.

Madison giggled and continued to massage him. With the continuous movement of her fingers over his ass, Gabe's cock stirred and all thoughts of her as just a masseuse disappeared. Once again she became Maddie Phillips, the woman he wanted to make love to.

"My hands are starting to hurt. I think I need to stop. Do you mind?"

"I was hoping you'd say that." Gabe rolled over onto his back and reached for her hand. "How did I get so lucky to have you in my life? You're wonderful, Maddie."

195

She smiled and pleasure flickered in her gaze, before her eyelashes swept down to cover it. Her soft features flickered in the firelight. God, he wanted her. In every way, not just in bed.

"Come here." Gabe pulled her back down next to him. She giggled and snuggled close to him. Her warm breath feathered over his chin. "You're so beautiful."

He lifted her chin so she met his gaze and closed his mouth over hers. Reaching down, he slid her silk nightgown up her body, his hand caressing each inch of skin he revealed.

"So soft," he murmured against her mouth. "Here." His fingers danced over the softness of her thigh. "And especially here."

He moved his hand to the silk panties between her legs and found the fabric soaked with her arousal. He hooked a finger on each side of her panties and pulled them from her body.

"You're so sexy here." He caressed the small swell of her belly and up to her aching breasts. He stroked her nipples until they tightened into firm peaks that he could take into his mouth. His tongue swirled over her, tasting and suckling.

"Gabe..." She sighed, running a hand down his chest and then lower to his erection.

He groaned when her fingers wrapped around him, burying his face against the curve of her neck, while she stroked him. Needing to touch her, he delved his fingers between her legs and inside her. The heat and wetness of her sheath finally drove him to the edge.

"Now, I need you now."

He sat up to put on the necessary protection and stared down at her.

The image of her lying on the fur riveted him. Her mouth swollen and parted, her legs spread and the lips of her sex shining with the moisture he'd brought forth.

But her eyes were the most amazing. They stared up at him with an expression of desire, tenderness, and complete trust.

Gabe knelt in front of her and hooked his hands under her knees, pulling her toward him. He slid her legs up over his shoulders, and entered her with one smooth thrust.

Her eyes closed and her mouth parted, and it was all he could do to keep control. But he did, thrusting slow and deep, and then increasing the pace.

He watched Maddie as her fingers gripped the fur blanket, her head thrown back. Her cries spurred him on, and he pushed harder into her. Each thrust brought a tightness in his chest and further bonded her to him.

With a ragged groan he came and her inner muscles clenched around him through his explosion. A second later she cried out with her own climax.

He lowered her legs back to the blanket and stroked a hand down her quivering stomach.

"I'll be right back." He stood and left her alone in the gentle flicker of firelight.

He disposed of the condom and went to grab another blanket. When he returned, Maddie waited for him exactly as he'd left her. She gave him a lazy smile and patted the fur next to her.

Gabe lay down and scooted close to her, pulling the blanket over their bodies. She snuggled against him and buried her face against his chest.

"Thank you, Maddie." His lips brushed over her forehead.

She kissed his chest in response.

He closed his eyes, listening to the crackling of the fire.

Chapter Nineteen

Gabe woke the next morning and listened to the sound of the rain coming down on the roof of the log cabin. The power hadn't yet come on and the soft light of early morning spilled through the windows. With the fire out, the room had turned drafty, but he didn't feel the cold with the fur blanket and the warmth of his woman in his arms.

His woman. Feathering a hand down her back, he pondered that thought. What a primal way of putting it. His caress became more possessive when he thought back to last night. It still blew his mind that she hadn't looked at him like he was some kind of monster when he told her about Ricky.

For the first time in his life, he realized, he was almost ready to forgive himself. No matter how many times in the past Eric or his aunt had told him to let it go, he'd always held onto that self-destructive guilt. And then Maddie had come and changed everything. There wasn't a single part of him she hadn't changed.

She stirred in his arms, nuzzling her cheek against his chest and emitting a soft sigh. Gabe dropped his chin to the top of her head and closed his eyes again.

He just lay there, listening to the rain and enjoying the feel of holding Maddie. The ringing of his cell finally encouraged him to get up.

Setting her gently aside, he slid out from the blanket and went to find his phone.

Madison woke to the sound of Gabe's voice. She stretched her body out under the blanket and enjoyed the sensual softness of the fur against her naked skin. A languid smile passed over her face. Had she ever been more relaxed and just plain happy?

Rolling onto her side, Madison watched him pace across the room. His expression became unreadable as he spoke to someone on his cell phone. He hadn't put on any clothes, which she didn't mind because it gave her the chance to admire his exquisite body. He was all sinewy muscle and strength. He seemed perfect. Her protector and lover.

He turned just then and saw her watching him. His expression softened as he looked at her and mouthed "good morning" while still listening to the caller.

She mouthed a greeting back and her smile widened.

She got up out of their makeshift bed and went to the bathroom to wash her face and brush her teeth. When she came back out, Gabe had his travel bag out and had begun packing up his things. She took in the scene and glanced back at him.

"What's going on?"

"We're going back to Seattle. Go ahead and pack up your stuff when you get the chance."

"Going back? But why—"

Her question was cut off as he hauled her into his arms and dropped a long, deep kiss on her mouth. When he raised his head she'd almost forgotten what she'd just asked.

"They've got him, Maddie."

She blinked and shook her head.

"They just brought the Espresso Bandit into custody."

Her breath caught in her throat. "Are...are you sure?"

"Yes." He went back to packing. "And they want you to identify him in a lineup at four. So we need to haul ass."

Her knees weakened and she sat on the couch. She should have been elated—and she was. But the elation collided with the knowledge that the intimacy of the past days would end.

"Maddie?" Gabe's expression had turned to one of concern.

"No, I'm fine." She shook her head. "It's just strange. I almost didn't think they were going to get him. It's weird knowing I don't have to be afraid anymore."

"Of course they got him." He sat beside her. "And everything can go back to normal now."

Her eyes widened at his words and he laughed, realizing his mistake.

"Okay, not everything."

"I was going to say..."

"Maddie, I'm not going anywhere." He squeezed her hand.

Madison's hand tightened in his and she nodded. "Thank you. Let me just throw my things together and we can head out."

On the drive home, Madison thought about what would happen next. Of course she'd reopen Ooo La Latté and hope that business would be good. Then there was the move back into her apartment to be made. No more waking up next to Gabe. The thought sent an empty feeling through her and built on the unease that was already present.

"What's wrong?"

She wasn't surprised that he'd picked up on her fluctuating mood.

"I'm not sure. Something just feels off," she admitted.

"Are you worried about identifying him?"

"I don't know." She shrugged and glanced out the window. "The whole thing feels surreal."

"Understandable. I'll be with you the whole time, *mi vida*. You don't have to worry about a thing." He went quiet for a moment. "We're running a little early. Do you want to grab some lunch?"

"Think we could swing by my apartment? I'm all out of clean clothes and I wouldn't mind grabbing a shower."

"Sure we can. I'll fix you something to eat while you're getting ready." He gave her a knowing smile. "You do have some type of food in those cupboards, right?"

"Give me some credit. I've got crackers and Top Ramen." Her nose crinkled. "But...I'm not sure how old they are. Does Top Ramen expire?"

He laughed. "I'll figure out something."

They pulled up at her apartment building a short while later. Gabe carried her suitcase as he followed her into the lobby.

"Want to take the stairs instead of the elevator?" Madison asked him. When he gave her an incredulous look she explained defensively, "Fine, I just thought we could use the exercise."

"I've got your twenty-pound suitcase in my hand. And besides, haven't I given you enough of a workout all week?"

Madison didn't think she was still capable of blushing, but her cheeks definitely felt warmer at his teasing smile.

"Point taken."

They took the elevator up to her floor and walked down the deserted hall to her apartment. She unlocked the door and stepped inside.

When she looked around she saw what Gabe must have seen the first time he'd come in. It was a total mess. Even in the short time that they'd lived together, she'd gotten used to what a clean home could look like. It was so much nicer to return to. She made a mental note to try to change her messy habits. And maybe even go to the store and buy some groceries that could actually go bad.

Madison shrugged off her sweater and tossed it onto the floor. She'd start the cleaning thing tomorrow.

"All right, I'm going to go and get that shower now. You're good for making us lunch?"

"I'm good," he verified and proceeded to explore the cupboards in her kitchen.

"Thanks, I'll be out in fifteen."

Standing under the onslaught of warm water, Madison smiled. She really was so fortunate to have Gabe. It was amazing how things had worked out between them.

She lathered her hair with shampoo and started singing at the top of her lungs, an old Rolling Stones song. She giggled, letting the freedom of not having to worry anymore roll over her.

Ten minutes later she wrapped a towel around herself and walked into the bedroom. She searched her wardrobe, bypassing the expensive brand-name clothes and picking her oldest and most comfortable pair of jeans. She slipped on a concert T-shirt she'd picked up from some rock band years ago, realizing she'd never even worn it once. Gabe would probably have a good laugh when he saw her. Speaking of which, it was awfully quiet in the other room.

"Gabe?" she called out as she slipped on her sandals.

There was no answer. Madison left her room to find him. Her glance darted around the kitchen, but he wasn't there. She looked toward the living room and then the hallway. Slowly, her gaze moved back to the living room, her mind registering what she'd just seen. Her body went numb and the room started to spin.

"You know," the man said conversationally from her couch. "You pretty much defiled that Rolling Stones song. Has anybody ever told you that you can't sing?"

Chapter Twenty

When she didn't respond, the man she knew only as the Espresso Bandit went on.

"I'm going to have to kill you for that, you know."

"You're going to kill me because I can't sing?" When Madison could finally speak her voice trembled.

"Well, no." He laughed and kept the gun trained on her. "Don't get me wrong, I am going to kill you. But not because of your singing."

"I see." Madison nodded. Not good. This was really not good. Where in the hell was Gabe? The hair on the back of her neck rose. She forced the question out. "What did you do with him?"

"Him?" The man raised an eyebrow. "Oh, your boyfriend? Nothing. He left about ten minutes ago."

Madison blinked in shock. Her stomach clenching like she'd been punched. Gabe had left her. He couldn't have. But deep down inside she knew the truth. He'd left her. The words looped in her head, keeping her from focusing on the situation at hand. Why? Why had Gabe left? She couldn't come up with one logical reason.

"Are you surprised?" the man asked. "Come on now, you women are always complaining about how men are such

204

bastards. Are you really shocked that one would leave you to fend for yourself?"

His words snapped Madison from her terror and shock. All thoughts of Gabe vanished and it became all too clear. If she was going to survive this, she was going to have to do it herself. Because nobody else was going to save her.

"Well, I see you're not going to be much fun." He sighed and stood, removing the safety on the gun.

"Hey, wait a minute." She put her hands up to stop him, her heart pounding as sweat broke out on the back of her neck. "There's no need to kill me. I mean, do you really have to? You could go across the border to Canada. I'll forget all about you and pretend this conversation never took place. I hear it's lovely up there. Ever been to Whistler?"

"I was thinking about it, actually." The man looked thoughtful. "But everything changed when the shop owner on Broadway died. The police are such sticklers about that kind of thing. They'd find me and extradite me."

Madison swallowed hard as her glance drifted around the room for a weapon. She spotted one by the couch. Trying to be casual, she walked slowly toward him.

He stepped in front of her. "What do you think you're doing?"

"Umm...if you don't mind, I'd like to sit down for a minute. I'm trying to come to terms with the fact that you're going to kill me."

The man obviously thought he had a sense of humor, so she tried to play on it.

"Besides if you shoot me on the couch, it'll leave less of a mess. My parents pay for this place and if you ruin the rug they won't get their deposit back."

"Hmm, interesting concept. I like the way you think." He gestured with the gun. "Go ahead and sit down."

"Thanks." She sat, not believing her good luck. Or how stupid he was. Her amazement grew when he actually moved to sit beside her. She could see that he seemed to be struggling a bit with his right arm, probably because Gabe had shot him there.

"So, before you kill me, why don't you do the *tell all* part. You know, where you brag about all the things you got away with, only you couldn't tell anyone because they were illegal."

"What's to tell?" He shrugged. "I robbed twelve coffee shops to pay off a gambling debt."

"A gambling debt?" Madison's fear mixed with anger now as she reached her hand as inconspicuously as possible down the side of the couch. "I'm going to die because of a gambling debt? Couldn't it at least have been for something nobler? Like to pay for someone's cancer treatment?"

The man laughed, genuinely amused. "Noble? This isn't a fairy tale, darling. Your knight isn't going to ride in on a white horse to save you."

Apparently not. She'd realized that five minutes ago. Her hand closed around the object she sought.

"Please don't kill me," she pleaded.

"Oh, Madison." He looked disappointed. "I had so much more respect for you. Don't beg for your life now."

"Beg for my life?" She forced a laugh. "I wasn't begging for my life, I was giving you one last chance."

She swung the two-pound dumbbell up and into the side of his head. He fell backwards from the impact with a curse and she ran toward the door. By the time she had it open, she heard him swear and struggle to come after her.

She screamed and ran down the hallway, knowing no one would hear her. This was an intimate complex; she only had one neighbor on this floor and he was in Jamaica for the month.

She heard the door to her apartment smash open and fear clogged thick in her chest. The elevator was right in front of her, but like hell was she going to push the button and stand there and wait for it. She ran for the stairs just as he fired the first shot.

She screamed again, waiting for pain, but none came. Images of an old Oprah episode flashed through her head. If someone shot at you, you weren't supposed to run in a straight line. If you ran from side to side, you were less of a target.

She started weaving from one side of the hallway to the other, even as she heard more shots being fired. There was no pain and she knew it was working, especially when he started to swear louder at her.

She reached the stairwell and swung open the door. Looking down the five floors of descending stairs, she would be dead if she tried to outrun him.

When the door shut behind her, she hid behind it. She would be in his blind spot when he opened the door. Her heart pounded double from the adrenalin rush, even as her senses became a great deal sharper.

The door swung open and the man ran through. Without hesitation she jumped him, using surprise and her weight to catch him off guard. He stumbled toward the railing and lost his balance, going halfway over.

He grabbed her T-shirt, halting his fall and jerking her forward. She toppled over the railing after him, just managing to grab onto the bars before she fell. The man's grasp on her shirt loosened and he slid down her leg, still clutching her calf

207

until they both dangled over the edge.

Madison screamed. The shrill sound resonated in the stairwell as she tried to kick him free. All that kept him from falling to his death was his grasp on her leg. She had both arms wrapped around the railing but slipped a little more with each passing second.

God, we're both going to die!

He must have lost his grip on her leg, because he slid further down her leg and suddenly only held onto her ankle. She heard a pop, followed by a fierce throbbing. Her scream turned into a mix of terror and pain. Oh God, whatever had happened to her foot wasn't good.

She heard another snap and all the weight on her foot disappeared. The man's horrified screams rang in her ears until there was a thud and all went quiet again. She glanced down, seeing her sandal was gone. The leather must've broken. Her gaze drifted farther down and she saw the man's body twisted and lying like a sack of potatoes, her broken sandal clutched in his hand.

She swallowed hard and closed her eyes against the horrific image.

"Help..." Her fingers slipped a little more from the railing.

No! I'm not going to die after everything else I've just survived!

Sweat broke out on her brow and raw frustration ate in her gut. Her fingers closed tighter over the railing and she gave a grunt of determination, swinging her leg toward the stairs. Her ankle burned as it connected with the railing. The first try she didn't make it up. The second, she did. Slowly, she managed to pull herself up and onto the stairs.

Only after she knew she was safe and no longer in danger did she let herself fall apart.

Chapter Twenty-One

Madison had curled up into a ball, shaking and crying when the police finally arrived.

Gabe pushed past them all, coming to kneel beside her.

"God, Maddie! Maddie, *mi vida*, I am so sorry." He tried to pull her into his arms.

An onslaught of emotions poured through her, anger being the strongest of them. Madison fought just as hard as she had when fighting for her life.

"Get away," she screamed, beating at his arms.

"Maddie, wait—"

"Where were you? You show up now? Now that I'm no longer in danger of dying? You left me, Gabe. He was going to kill me. I was all alone and he was going to kill me!"

"Maddie, I got a phone call—"

"You promised me you'd be there for me," she cried hysterically. "You promised to protect me! Why weren't you there, Gabe? When I needed you most, why weren't you there?"

"Christ, will you let me explain." He groaned as he tried again to pull her against him. "I came as soon as I figured it out—"

"Let go," Madison screamed.

Finally another officer interceded and pulled Gabe away from her. He leaned close and said something into his ear. Gabe's mouth tightened, but he finally turned and walked away.

"Ma'am." The officer came and knelt beside her. "Is there someone we can call for you?"

With the distance between her and Gabe, she managed to compose herself enough to nod. "My mom."

"All right." He put a gentle hand under her elbow and helped her stand. "I have a daughter your age, you know. I wouldn't want her to be alone at a time like this. Let's go back into your apartment and you can sit down and wait for her."

She followed him, almost in a trance. Her head still swirled with the horrific images of what had happened. When he turned her toward the couch, she shook her head.

"Not there. I don't ever want to see that couch again." She moved instead into her bedroom and fell down onto the bed. "When my family comes, please send them to me."

"I will, Miss Phillips," the officer replied quickly. "You just let me know if you need anything."

"Thank you."

Gabe paced the hallway, fists clenched, jaw tight, worry and guilt tearing at his gut.

"How is she?" he demanded of his superior when he came out of her apartment.

"Pretty much in shock," the man replied and stroked his jaw. "She has some strong feelings against something that happened on the couch."

Gabe's eyes snapped shut as another wave of guilt and self-disgust washed over him. "It's my fault."

"You're not to blame, Martinez. Hell, Danica fell for it too. She's the one who gave him your number when he called in. In any case, you got us back here as soon as you figured it out. Things could have turned out a lot worse."

"I should have realized that it wasn't Valentino calling from the precinct this morning. But he confirmed all the information. He sounded so authentic." Gabe shook his head grimly. "And then he called me again to get me out of the apartment, so he could have her alone. Shit! How? How can this not be my fault?"

"Valentino's a rookie. Half the precinct still doesn't know who he is. He had his ID stolen on Monday, and I'm sure it's safe to say that the Bandit probably stole it." The older man's tone gentled. "Why don't you take the rest of the evening off, Martinez. We'll wrap things up and direct the M.E. when he gets here."

"I don't want to leave her," Gabe argued fiercely, jerking away from the hand the older man had put on his shoulder.

"I know you don't. But your presence seems to be causing further distress to Ms. Phillips. I understand how you're feeling, but please, just go with me on this one. I'm sure she'll come around."

Gabe's jaw flexed and finally he gave a terse nod. "All right. Thank you, sir."

He turned to walk down the stairs before realizing that the area had been taped off around the body. His gaze hardened on the crumpled figure of the dead man. If Maddie hadn't completed the job, Gabe would have killed the man himself.

Maddie...his chest tightened and he fought the urge to go back and find her, and to hell with his orders. God, would she ever forgive him?

"Can I bring you some tea, darling?"

Madison looked up at her mother almost in surprise. Her family had arrived an hour ago and stayed by her side while the police questioned her. She had finally gone numb from it all and tonelessly relayed answers to the questions they threw at her.

The older officer was nice. He'd been the one to make Gabe leave. The thought of Gabe made some flicker of emotion penetrate her numbed mind, but she quickly pushed it aside.

"I'm sorry, what did you say?" Madison asked as her mother continued to stare at her.

"Tea, Madison," her mother asked again gently. "I was wondering if you'd care for some."

"Sure."

She didn't drink tea. Her mother knew that. She was a coffee lover, but right now it seemed completely trivial and easier just to accept the tea.

Eric sat in the corner of her room, giving her a long and considering look.

"What is it, Eric?" she finally asked, sensing he wanted to say something.

"I was wondering why Gabe isn't here with you."

Trust him to get straight to the point. Madison's eyes narrowed slightly and a twinge of anger and pain finally penetrated.

"Because I didn't want him here."

"Do you blame him for what happened?" he asked without censuring the disapproval in his voice.

Madison didn't answer right away. "I don't know."

Eric stood and walked toward the bed, where she sat propped up against pillows. He dropped a slip of paper onto her lap.

She lowered her gaze. Picking it up, she read it through. It was from Gabe, saying he'd gotten an urgent page to come to the precinct as soon as possible. It told her to meet him there ASAP after her shower.

"It was on the fridge."

Madison handed him back the slip of paper. "I guess this would explain why he left me."

"He would never have intentionally put you in harm's way, Madison." Eric sat beside her. "In all the years I've known Gabe, I've never seen him look at a woman the way he looks at you."

Her head jerked up and she met her brother's probing stare.

"So you figured it out? We tried to hide it at the restaurant."

"I know you both better than that. Did you think I'd disapprove? You could do a lot worse than Gabe. He's a good guy. The parents would be thrilled, too." Eric's mouth twisted into a brief smile.

Madison's heart sped up even as she dropped her gaze. "It wasn't serious, Eric. Just a fling."

"He only had eyes for you on Monday night. Are you sure he sees it in the same light?"

"It doesn't matter anymore." She gave a weary shrug.

"Madison, we need to talk about something that happened a while ago. Something that—"

"Here's your tea, darling." Her mother entered the room carrying a cup of tea in a Tinkerbell mug, and a few saltine crackers.

Eric's expression turned frustrated and he stood, walking back to the window. Obviously he wasn't about to keep up this

213

conversation with their mother in the room.

"Did you know that you're out of food?" her mother asked. "I swear that tea must be as old as you are, and I had to fight off a mouse for those crackers."

That finally pulled a smile from Madison. "Funny, Mom. I plan on going to the store sometime soon."

Her mother laced her hands together and glanced down at her daughter, biting her lip. "Actually, Madison, I've been speaking to your father in the other room. We were thinking that it might be best if you came to stay with us for a while."

Madison made a noise of surprise, and thought about the offer. The last place she wanted to stay was in this apartment. She couldn't look around without reliving it all. Maybe going back to her parents' home wouldn't be such a bad thing until she could find another place.

"All right. I'll come home."

"Wonderful. When you finish up with your tea, we'll take you over to Dr. Burton and have him look at your foot."

Madison lifted the tea and took a tentative sip, then set it down resolutely.

"Let's just go now. I can't stay here any longer."

ℰ

Gabe gripped the remote control in his hand, staring at the television that had started showing the evening news. The death of the Espresso Bandit was the top story. When they flashed Maddie's picture across the screen, he hurled the remote to the wall in frustration. He didn't care that it broke open and fell to the ground in pieces.

Damn it, he should be with her right now. He grabbed his

cell phone and punched in Eric's number.

"Hey, Gabe," Eric answered wearily.

"Eric. How is she?"

"She's getting her ankle plastered. It was broken in the struggle."

Gabe took a deep breath. God, he would have done anything to spare her this.

"Is she...is she asking for me?"

Eric didn't respond for a few seconds. "You know that I'll call you as soon as she does."

His gut twisted and he felt a bit sick. She hadn't yet asked for him. The words were unspoken and unneeded. If she hadn't asked for him by now, she probably wouldn't. The fragile trust they'd established over the last week and a half had snapped. It was totally gone.

"Gabe, you there?"

"I'm here."

"Look, don't take it personally. Give her some time," Eric advised. "If you haven't heard from her in a week, why don't you drop by my parents' house? She'll be staying with them."

The end of the week sounded like an impossible amount of time to wait. But he knew he would wait however long it took. He'd do anything to get her back.

"Fine. Thanks, Eric."

"No problem."

Gabe disconnected the call and stared at the television again. The newscasters had already moved on to the weather.

He got off the couch and went to find his keys. Just sitting around was driving him crazy—he needed to do something. Working out had always been a good distraction before; maybe it would do the same now. Somehow he doubted it, though.

℘

Sunday afternoon, Madison sat at a table on the balcony of her parents' house, drinking coffee and taking in the sunshine. The *Seattle Times* sat untouched next to her. She stared at the view of Seattle, trying not to think about what had happened almost a week ago.

The reporters hadn't stopped calling, asking for interviews. She still had no desire to grant one. It was all too fresh, the wound too raw.

The quietness of the morning suited her. She'd been left alone in the house, since her parents had gone to attend an early morning church service. But she wouldn't be alone for long. Eric had promised to drop by later with Lannie.

As if her thoughts had summoned them sooner, she heard the electric gate to their house closing. Madison took another sip of coffee and waited for them to find her.

Five minutes later, she nearly dropped her mug when Gabe walked out onto the balcony.

She stood quickly, setting the mug down with shaking hands.

"How did you get in here?"

Gabe lifted a brow and gave her a sardonic look. "Through the front gate. Your folks haven't changed the code recently."

Madison wondered briefly what was in the large envelope he carried, and glanced down at the table.

Oh God, it's too soon. I can't face him yet.

She took a deep breath and counted to ten. *Get some*

control, Maddie. Don't look like a terrified, weak woman.

Lifting her head, she felt the calm descend upon her.

Chapter Twenty-Two

Gabe knew the moment she put up the wall. The raw reaction in her eyes had disappeared, being replaced by something less vulnerable.

He let his gaze travel over her, noting that once again she was dressed in clothes that likely cost more than his paycheck. The only exception was her lack of designer heels. The cast was a deterrent, and instead she wore a sequined flip-flop on the uninjured foot.

"What brings you by, Gabe?" She gave him a polite smile as she gestured to the empty seat next to hers. "And why don't you sit down?"

What brought him by? Was she kidding? Gabe sat, never taking his gaze off her.

"Can I get you something to drink?" She started to hobble toward the door. "Some water? Soda?"

"Sit down, Maddie," Gabe said, more sharply than he'd intended. "I'm not here for a beverage."

She sank back down in her seat and picked up her own coffee. "Okay, I'll ask again. What are you here for, Gabe?"

"We need to talk about things. The most important thing being our relationship."

Something flickered in her gaze, before she lowered her

lashes. "Do we have a relationship? Last I understood, we weren't putting any labels on it."

"You know damn well we did, whether we put a fucking label on it or not."

"Actually." Madison crossed her legs and her skirt rose up an inch, exposing her smooth thigh. "I'm not so sure. I've been going over a few things in my head...and I'm wondering if maybe I mistook what we had for something else."

Not liking her tone, Gabe jerked his gaze from her thighs and met her uncertain gaze.

"I have a theory. One that came to me after I had to save myself on Tuesday." She took a deep breath. "You see, in the short time that we were together, I came to see you as my protector. Someone who would always be there for me."

"I wanted to be, Maddie. You know I would have given anything—"

"I know, Gabe. But let me finish. Things just got crazy that day, and suddenly I had to save myself."

She might has well have been throwing knives, for her words couldn't have hurt more. He swallowed against the rawness in his throat. "I made a mistake, Maddie. I tried to get back to you in time. I brought half the damn force—"

"I know you did, Gabe." She held up a hand to stop him. "And I'm not blaming you. Really, I'm not."

"Aren't you? It sure as hell sounds like it. But, please, go on." His jaw worked with frustration. Morbid curiosity was the only thing that made him want to hear what she had to say next.

"I'm just not sure that what we had was more than...was more than a little hero worship combined with good old-fashioned lust."

He blinked, his stomach clenching. She couldn't believe that. Not anymore than he did.

His voice was harsh. "Bullshit. You're just afraid."

"I'm afraid?" Panic and doubt flared in her gaze. Then anger darkened her eyes, and her mouth grew tight. "Afraid is what I was the day someone tried to kill me. I've already experienced the most terrifying thing a person can go through. Why would I be afraid of sex?"

"It's not about sex, Maddie."

"Isn't it? And look, you don't need to worry about me being pregnant. I took a test and I'm not." She stood and he could see the way her hands trembled. "I don't think we should talk about this anymore. Maybe you should just see yourself out."

Gabe stood and grasped her elbow and swung her around into his arms.

"*Stop.* This won't solve anything." She attempted to push him away, but he'd already lowered his mouth to hers.

She struggled for only a second before her body yielded to his. Her soft moan was all it took to undo him. He placed his hands around her waist and lifted her easily onto the table, not even breaking the kiss for a moment. Madison unfastened his shirt and had her fingers inside it, stroking over his chest.

He groaned, unable to suppress the quiver that ran through him. God, it felt so good to have her back in his arms. To have her not fight him. And even if for only a moment, to have her not hate him.

He spread her thighs and stepped between them, pulling her shirt off and dragging her bra down off her breasts.

"Someone might see us," she protested weakly, covering herself.

Gabe gently grasped her wrists and pulled them away from

her breasts. "Nobody can see onto your porch—the angle's not right."

He closed his mouth around one of her nipples, loving the choked sound she made. Her fingers jerked in his hair, holding his head to her breast. He suckled on her gently and moved one hand under her skirt. Reaching the thin cotton barrier of her panties, he massaged one finger against the fabric and into her wet warmth.

Madison groaned and grabbed at his shoulder.

"I've got to taste you again," Gabe muttered, dropping to his knees. "Remind myself you're alive."

He pulled her forward to the edge of the table and lowered his mouth to the cotton of her panties. He licked and sucked through the fabric, teased by the musky scent and hint of moisture. His tongue stroked over her cleft, causing her panties to sink further in, and they immediately became soaked.

He needed more. Gabe hooked his fingers under the waistband of her panties and slid them down her legs and off.

The sight of her plump, wet folds was so erotic his cock went rock hard.

Placing a thumb on each side of her lips, he parted her and blew gently on the moisture inside. He pushed a finger into her tight channel and then retreated, using the slippery moisture to stroke over her clitoris.

"Gabe..." She moaned and her legs fell open even further.

He toyed with her clit, watching as it swelled under his touch. He leaned forward, pressing his face into her again and licked up and into her cleft.

Madison jerked against him, but he held her still, dipping his tongue again and again into her slippery channel. He dragged it back to her clit to circle and flick against it before finally sucking the swollen bud into his mouth.

Gabe heard her guttural groan and answered by pushing two fingers inside her, penetrating her while he brought her to a climax in his mouth.

With her thighs still shaking from the orgasm, he stood and kissed the side of her neck. He let his gaze meet her passion-clouded eyes.

"Maddie," he murmured, stroking her cheek. "I've missed you, *mi vida*. Don't you see how wrong it is to try to fight this?"

The tiny smile on Madison's face slipped and she closed her eyes. "Oh, Gabe...I want you in my bed, obviously I do. But as for more than that? I'm just not sure."

Her words were like a bucket of cold water on his desire for her. He released her so abruptly she had to grab the table to keep from falling.

"Fine, Madison. Have it your way. But I won't be just some guy you fuck when you're horny."

She winced, already pulling her clothes back on. "Gabe, wait. That came out wrong. I just need more time to think about things."

"At least have the decency to be straight with me," he ground out. "This goes beyond the relationship label. You aren't ready to forgive me for what happened Tuesday. I broke your trust and now you're afraid. I'm sorry I let you down, Maddie. But I'm human."

"Gabe—"

"I wish I could've been the knight in shining armor you wanted me to be. But I wasn't. And now, unfortunately, I'll never measure up to the kind of perfection you expect."

He turned and strode back into the house, leaving her alone on the balcony, so blinded by his emotions that he almost rammed into Eric, who walked down the hallway.

"Gabe." Eric put a hand out to steady him. "Did you come to see Madison?"

"Yeah, and now I'm leaving."

Eric held fast to Gabe's arm, refusing to let him walk away.

"I told you to give her a week." Eric's gaze softened with sympathy.

Gabe issued a harsh laugh. "Somehow, I doubt two more days would've made much of a difference. Let me pass, Eric. I don't want to stick around where I'm not wanted."

"All right," Eric released him with obvious reluctance. "I still think she just needs time."

"It doesn't matter anymore."

"She cares about you."

"I don't think so."

"Hey, hold on a second." Eric again stopped him as he went to move past. "Don't forget the rehearsal dinner on Friday night."

"I'm leaving town for the week, and I'm turning off my phone. But I'll be there Friday," Gabe promised, and walked out of the house.

Madison hadn't stopped shaking when her brother came out on the porch a few minutes later.

"So, that's it then?" Eric pulled out a chair and sat across from her. "You're just going to write him off?"

Her stomach clenched and she averted her gaze to the view. "I don't know, Eric. I'm so screwed up emotionally right now."

"It wasn't his fault."

"I know it wasn't."

"Do you? Deny it all you want, but it sure seems like you're blaming him."

"Fine. You know what? Maybe I am." She squeezed her eyes shut, frustration making her voice louder. "I'm tired of it all. My entire life you guys have shielded me, protected me to the point where I felt smothered. But when it came down to it, no one could keep me safe. I still had to save my own ass in the end." She threw her hands up in the air. "And you know? I'm done. I don't want to be dependent on anyone, anymore."

"Maddie..."

Her eyes snapped open. The tone in his voice had changed, and he'd called her by the nickname she'd dropped years ago.

"There are reasons why we were overprotective." His voice gentled. "I'm sure you don't remember it, but something happened when you were just a little kid. Something bad."

Her gut clenched as she stared at him for a moment. "What do you mean something bad?"

"Do you have any memories, scary memories from your childhood?"

"What? Not that I remember..." Her eyebrows drew together and she shook her head. Something tickled the back of her mind.

Nightmares. She'd been plagued with them as a kid for the longest time before they grew less frequent and then finally stopped all together. For the life of her, she couldn't remember what they were about. She'd forgotten all about them until now.

Madison swallowed hard. "What happened to me, Eric? And why don't I know about it?"

Eric sighed and looked away. "You were abducted when you were three years old."

A vision flashed through her head so fast she could barely

hold onto it. Being tied up and thrown in the trunk of a car. Then thick darkness and absolute terror.

Sweat broke out over her body, even as a chill moved down her spine. "I was...abducted?"

"Some guy who worked for Dad decided he and his wife would kidnap you and hold you for ransom. You were missing for almost a week."

Shock rendered her speechless.

"Honestly, I don't remember much. I was only eight, and Mom and Dad made me promise to never talk about it once you came home."

"So they paid the ransom?"

"I don't think so. I think the police went in and found you during a raid. They figured out who'd taken you."

She finally closed her jaw, which seemed to have lost all gravity. The nightmares, the seemingly ridiculous fear of car trunks...they must have originated from the kidnapping. *Kidnapping.* Her head spun and she pressed her palm against her forehead.

"I don't know what to say. I wish you had told me. It would have made more sense, and I wouldn't have resented the protectiveness as much."

"Come on. This is Maddie Phillips we're talking about. You would have gotten frustrated whether you knew or not. You're the most independent woman I know."

She nodded, a weak smile playing around her lips. "You're right. I would have still been frustrated."

"I shouldn't have told you. The parents would rip me a new one if they knew I'd told you. But I know you can handle it now." He paused. "And I want you to stop coming down so hard on Gabe."

The mention of Gabe had her stomach in knots and regret piercing her.

"He kept you safe, what, ninety-nine percent of the time?" He raised an eyebrow skeptically. "The Espresso Bandit was slick, Madison. You can't blame Gabe for the one time he didn't protect you."

"Eric..." she protested, not wanting to hear this right now. Not with trying to digest what had happened to her when she was a toddler.

"No, you need to hear this, Madison. Besides the kidnapping, nothing bad has ever happened to you. We made sure of it. But there was bound to be a time where one of us couldn't protect you. And it just happened to fall on Gabe's watch."

She closed her eyes, gnawing on her lip. He was right. Eric was totally right. But then he always had a habit of seeing the bottom line. *Even when I'm too stubborn to.*

"So what do I do?" Her voice grew hoarse. "He hates me now. He has to. I treated him like..."

"Shit? Yeah, Madison, you did." Eric grabbed her hand and gave it a reassuring squeeze. "But I'd wager my next paycheck that he loves you. And if you make things right, you guys can move past this."

Her pulse doubled. He thought Gabe might be in love with her? Could it be true? Warmth spread through her body, and she grew dizzy with the possibility.

"I will. I'll make things right." And she wanted to. Now. Not tomorrow. Not in ten minutes when her brother left. But now.

She grabbed her purse, fumbling for her cell phone.

Eric laughed softly. "You'll have to wait, Madison."

She jerked her gaze up, almost desperate to fix things.

"Why? Why do I have to wait? I need to make this right. I need to do it now."

"Gabe's leaving town for a while. And he's turned off his phone."

"What? How do you know?"

"He told me when I ran into him in the house." Eric gave her a gentle smile. "Take some time. Think about this and make sure it's what you really want. You'll see him on Friday night at the rehearsal dinner."

Friday night. God, it was like five days away. She closed her eyes and nodded. Once again, he was right, though. She did need time to think this through.

"Thank you, Eric."

"You're welcome. Now get yourself together, the parents will be home soon."

$$\mathcal{SO}$$

Madison held her second grand opening for Ooo La Latté on Thursday morning. She unlocked the door with shaking hands and went inside, locking it again behind her.

She leaned against the glass with a shaky sigh. A part of her was still terrified by the idea of being back. Running a hand through her hair, she let her gaze move over her shop.

This is my future. Whether or not Gabe decided to take her back, she would always have her shop.

Gabe...her heart twisted at the thought of him and that moment on the balcony. This week had been hell on her nerves. And the more she thought about it, the more she realized she was in love with him. And tomorrow night she'd find out if he felt the same.

Madison pushed away from the door and hit the light switch. Walking past all the tables and couches, she went straight behind the counter.

She ignored the acidic feeling in her stomach as her fingers traced over the groove in the wall where a bullet had recently been imbedded. The bullet that had been intended for her. That would have hit her, had it not been for Gabe.

Someone knocked on the glass door, and she jumped in surprise, her heart thudding like crazy in her chest.

Madison glanced toward the entrance, but since it was still early in the morning, darkness still lingered outside. Wiping her damp palms on her pants, she moved slowly to the door.

It was Sarah, her arms folded across her chest as she shivered in the drizzle.

Madison twisted the lock and pulled open the door. "Hey, you. I can't tell you how glad I am that you came back."

"What can I say? The pay's great," Sarah replied with a grin and slid past her. "And you're famous now, so that makes me famous by association."

Madison laughed, letting some of the tension drain away. "Infamous is more like it. But I think it'll do wonders for business. And we'll need to do some serious catch-up."

"No kidding." Sarah sat on one of the leather chairs and pulled off her jacket. "So, really...are you doing all right, Madison?"

Madison sat across from her and shrugged. "As well as can be expected, I guess. But I'm ready to be back. And I'll just take it a day at a time."

"That's all you can do. And I have to warn you that there's a media van out front."

"I know." Madison ran a hand through her hair and smiled.

"I told the reporter hello and promised to bring him out a cappuccino."

Sarah stood with a laugh. "You're going to be just fine, Madison. We'd better get ready if we're going to open soon."

"Yeah, good call."

The morning flew by. There were times they were so busy the line formed out the door. Of course the constant media presence was probably most of the draw. But if it brought in new customers, Madison wasn't about to complain.

After lunch, the rush started to diminish. Madison went into the back to rest her feet and eat some food. As she munched on celery and hummus, she stared at the envelope that sat on her desk. The same envelope Gabe had left with her two days ago. He'd left so fast that he hadn't taken it with him. Then again, maybe he hadn't intended to.

She'd glanced inside, seen the photos, and closed it again. Then spent the next hour in another crying episode.

Madison set down a stick of celery and picked up the envelope again. She pulled the eight-by-ten photos out and started gingerly flipping through them.

The one that caught her attention was the photo of herself. It was the one Gabe had taken at the beach on Whidbey. A beautiful black and white shot, close enough to see the whimsical expression on her face and the blur of mountains behind her.

Just looking at the photo made her feel warm inside. Not only was it an excellent photograph, but the image evoked memories of how happy she'd been that day.

Madison put the rest of the photos back in the envelope, but kept the image of herself out. She set it on the shelf above her desk. Jeez, he had talent. If he forgave her, she'd really push him to display his work in her shop.

She picked up her coffee and took another sip before returning to the front of the store. Her gaze went straight to the man facing away from her in a police uniform. Her pulse quickened, and she grabbed onto the counter to steady herself.

"Brian!" Sarah ran past her and went to wrap her arms around the man.

It wasn't Gabe. Madison experienced such crushing disappointment that it became hard to breathe.

Of course it wasn't Gabe. She'd pretty much told Gabe to go to hell. Why would he be in her store?

"Madison?" Sarah came hurrying back to where Madison gripped the counter. "I'm going to take my lunch now."

"Have fun," Madison called, but Sarah was already halfway out the door. She glanced around the shop—empty except for a couple of customers who were working on laptops and drinking coffee.

Madison knew if she stayed stagnant, her mind would go back to Gabe, and her brain was already fried with too many painful memories.

Tomorrow. Tomorrow she'd make things right.

She headed back to the espresso counter, deciding it wouldn't hurt to practice making drinks.

∞

Madison got ready for the rehearsal dinner with care. She wanted to look good. Damn good. When she laid her heart on the table and begged for forgiveness, she wanted to look good doing it.

She hadn't been able to shake the slight depression that had taken hold lately. Her shop was up and running, and raking in a ton of money. But even with the success of her business, she wasn't happy. There was one thing missing in her life. Or better yet, one person.

She slipped a little black dress over lacy black lingerie, and her thoughts reluctantly touched back on her encounter with Gabe last Sunday.

How had she ever thought she could use him for just a casual fling, as a way to cleanse her dating palate? She'd been ridiculously naïve on that one.

Her thoughts turned to some of the things he'd said after he made love to her on the patio. About her expectations for a knight in shining armor. He'd really hit a nerve. Because that's exactly what she had expected of him.

Which was totally unrealistic for the average man of flesh and blood. Her life wasn't some medieval romance novel. And even if it had been, she probably would've ended up dying of the plague. Now that was reality.

Her talk with Eric had also helped her realize how off her reasoning had been.

Tonight. Tonight things would be made right. Her pulse raced with sudden nerves as she put on a pair of long silver earrings.

She went to find her shoes and winced. Now there was one area where she wouldn't be making any fashion statements. Her right foot was still in a cast, so she'd been wearing flats or flip-flops all week on the left one. After scowling at her choices, she finally decided on the sequined black flip-flop again.

She glanced at her watch and swore softly. Well, damn it. She was already running late. Rushing her makeup, she grabbed her purse and hurried out the door as fast as her wounded foot would allow her to.

"You're late, Madison," Eric called from the front of the room as she rushed down the aisle.

The wedding had been booked in an old, elegant hotel. The ballroom turned into an enchanting location for the wedding.

All the bridesmaids and groomsmen were lined up to run through the ceremony. She averted her gaze from Gabe, too nervous to even look, though she could see him out of her peripheral vision. Everyone stared at her as she made her way down the aisle.

"Sorry," she mumbled and hurried to take her spot. Or at least what she assumed to be her spot since it was the only gap in the lineup.

The pastor cleared his throat and went on explaining what would happen next in the ceremony.

Madison's gaze lifted to the man across from her. Her match in the lineup, likely. She had no idea who he was, but he blatantly leered at her and the expression in his eyes went beyond flirting.

She turned away from him and looked around at the line of men and women. Oh God. Now wonder she was attracting so much attention. While everyone else was dressed in jeans and even sweatpants, she had decked herself out to the hilt.

Oh, why hadn't she taken the word rehearsal a little more literally?

Her posture slumped a bit and she did her best to appear invisible. She finally looked over at Gabe and saw the look of disapproval directed at her. Great, and obviously she was off to a good start with him too.

They'd have time to talk during the dinner. She turned away from his censuring gaze and listened to the pastor.

An hour later they were done with the long and drawn out

rehearsal, and had caravanned over to a nearby restaurant for dinner.

Her parents had rented out the entire restaurant, which included an expensive buffet of food, along with an open bar to please everyone.

Since the wedding party consisted of sixteen people—not including the bride and groom—the atmosphere in the room had grown fairly rowdy.

Madison sat at a table fiddling with an uneaten piece of shrimp, and stared at Gabe across the room. She'd finally gotten the nerve to approach him earlier, but Christy had sat beside him. They'd been inseparable the rest of the night. He hadn't even tried to speak to her once.

Her head felt heavy, her throat tight, and tears were just barely held at bay.

And what did you expect? For him to beg you for a second chance? Again? You're the one who needs to apologize, Madison, not him.

But still, he'd certainly moved on fast enough. Maybe he wasn't in love with her. Men in love didn't go off and flirt with other women.

She watched as Christy placed a hand on his arm and said something into his ear. He smiled at her and leaned down to reply.

Suddenly nauseous, Madison stood, needing to go outside and get some air.

"Hey, sexy, I brought you a drink."

Madison glanced up to see the groomsman she'd been partnered up with. Lannie's cousin, apparently.

"I don't drink," she replied automatically. Her gaze once again found Gabe, and she watched as Christy slipped an arm around his waist and urged him onto the small dance floor.

"On second thought, give it to me," she muttered and snatched the frothy pink drink from him. She downed half of it in one swallow.

"Not bad for a girl who doesn't drink." The man gave her an admiring glance.

She offered him a bland smile. What was his name again? Oh, yes, John. What a creep.

"Hey, aren't you the chick who killed the Espresso Bandit by throwing him down a flight of stairs?" he asked suddenly.

Madison downed the rest of the drink and handed him the empty glass. Choosing not to answer, she instead asked, "Could you get me another one?"

John gave a long whistle. "Damn, that was hot. You bet I'll get you another. Hang on a second, sexy, and I'll be right back."

Just another Ivy League asshole. She shook her head as he disappeared. Madison ran a hand over her forehead and realized the alcohol had already hit her. Maybe that second drink wasn't such a good idea. Her tolerance level had always been low, but after a drunken night in Italy that had her dancing naked on a bar, she'd sworn off alcohol for good.

"Madison, darling." Her parents were suddenly standing in front of her. "We're going to head out now and leave the partying to you younger ones."

Madison frowned. She'd forgotten they were even here. It was a good thing they were leaving. The last thing they needed was to see their respectable daughter get trashed at the rehearsal dinner.

"All right, have a good night."

Then they were gone and John returned with her second drink. By the time she finished it, things were starting to look up.

She still couldn't stand to see Gabe and Christy getting cozy in the corner, but had grown a little more numb and relaxed by now.

"Hey, sexy, let's dance." John grabbed her hand and pulled her onto the floor.

She thought about protesting, but decided it would take too much energy. She pulled back slightly and proceeded to dance, but more with herself than with him.

They were playing the disco standard "I Will Survive", and suddenly she knew it must be meant for her. This song was her theme song. So she started to sing it. Loudly.

She didn't notice when John disappeared from her side, just kept spinning on her good foot and shouting the words at the top of her lungs.

Suddenly an arm wrapped around her waist. She was jerked to a stop and pulled up against a hard body.

"Hey, wait a minute," she grumbled and opened her eyes to see Gabe scowling down at her. "Oh, hello."

Chapter Twenty-Three

"Are you drunk, Maddie?" Gabe frowned. Hadn't she told him before that she never drank?

"Hmm. I couldn't tell you for sure. I've had two pink things, and I certainly feel more relaxed. But would I classify myself as drunk? Well, maybe, but—"

"I thought you didn't drink." He sighed, pulling her more firmly against him as she lost her balance. It felt good to have her in his arms, even if it was only because she was drunk.

"Oh, I don't drink," she protested. "I just had a couple of pink things."

"Don't you think that maybe you should stop with the alcohol?"

"Not really. Because I've noticed that the more I drink, the less I feel." She laughed and threw her arms in the air with delight. "And you don't know how great it is to not feel."

"Christ, Maddie," he growled against her ear, his arms tightening around her waist to keep her upright. "You're making a spectacle of yourself. Try to remember that you're at your brother's rehearsal dinner."

Her face flushed red, and he could tell he'd embarrassed and hurt her. "Oh, don't be so damn uptight." She pushed at him until he finally had to let her go or risk even more of a scene. "Go find Christy. I'm sure she's missing you right now."

He didn't give a damn about Christy. He wanted to drag Maddie out of the restaurant and back to his place. Take her to bed and make love to her until they both couldn't see straight. Not that she'd ever let him that close to her again.

He watched her walk away from him, or limp, to be more accurate. His frown deepened as he saw the man who'd been plying her with drinks approach her again.

"Gabe." Christy appeared beside him. "I was wondering where you'd gone off to. Aren't you sweet to check up on Eric's sister? You're such a nice guy."

Gabe cast her a sideways glance. He couldn't do it anymore—lead this woman on. Really he'd only engaged in the flirting as a balm to his wounded ego, and maybe make Madison jealous. Unfortunately, it hadn't done either. And, worst of all, it was completely unfair to Christy.

His gaze once again found Maddie and John. They were sitting at a table and she had another drink in her hand. With the wedding in a little over twelve hours, she couldn't afford to get drunk enough to have a hangover. But maybe it was already too late for that.

"Do you want to dance, Gabe?" Christy asked, and gave him a thoughtful smile. "Or maybe...we could get out of here and find someplace more private."

Gabe's attention again returned to Christy. A month ago, he would have been all over her invitation. She was sexy and sweet, and charming enough to tempt any man.

"I'm sorry, Christy." Gabe took her hand and gave it a small squeeze. "I haven't been very up-front with you. There's kind of someone else—"

"Madison." She sighed and looked away. "Oh, don't look so surprised. I don't usually hit on taken men, but when I asked her if you two were together at dinner a couple of weeks ago, she said you weren't. I thought I'd give it a try. Lannie thought we'd be great together."

Gabe shifted awkwardly and started to say something.

"But honestly, you're not really my type anyway," Christy went on quickly with an overly bright smile. "I was just trying to make Lannie happy. She's forever harping on me to get myself a man."

"I think it's a requirement of friends to harp," he replied and turned again to look at Maddie, but she'd disappeared. "If you'll excuse me."

"Of course," she murmured and stepped away.

Gabe pushed his way through the intoxicated wedding party, looking around for any sign of Maddie. But she had disappeared, along with any trace of John. He ran out the side exit to see if they might've stepped outside, and that's when he saw her.

John was in the process of urging her to get into the passenger seat of his car, which he'd pulled up to the curb.

By the time he reached them, Maddie had sat in the bucket seat of the sports car.

"What are you doing?" Gabe demanded, grabbing the door before John could shut it and lock her inside.

"She's a little tired, so I'm taking her home." John had the decency to flush.

"My ass, you are. I seriously doubt you've got her best interests in mind right now."

"Excuse me? I don't see how this is any of your concern." John's nostrils flared. "She's obviously going with me willingly."

"Yeah, because you got her drunk," Gabe snapped with disgust, reaching down to pull Maddie from the car.

"What's going on?" She blinked at him, so out of it that she didn't even seem to realize what had happened.

"Hey, back off, man." John made a move to block him. "She wants to go with me."

"Yeah? Then ask her again tomorrow when she's sober. If she still wants to go home with you, then she will." He swung Maddie up into his arms, and she giggled as if it were the funniest thing ever. "It's pretty pathetic when you have to get a woman drunk so she'll go home with you."

"Yeah? Well, who asked you anyway?"

John got into his tiny sports car, slammed the door, and sped off.

Satisfied that the other man had left, Gabe adjusted his grip on Maddie, making his way back toward his car. She seemed to pick that moment to have a flash of clarity.

"Where are we going?"

"I'm taking you home," he responded curtly.

"Home?" She began to struggle. "I'm not going home, I'm having fun. Put me down!"

Gabe tightened his grip and ignored her protests, instead managing to get her buckled into the passenger seat of his car.

"In case you've forgotten, Maddie, we're scheduled to be in a wedding in the morning."

"But that's not until tomorrow! It's Friday night, Gabe." She frowned even as she laid her head against the seat and closed her eyes.

"You'll thank me in the morning for getting you safely home and in your own bed."

"You're not taking me to my apartment, are you?" she asked, her eyes snapping open.

"That's where I planned on heading—"

"No! Please, don't take me back there. I don't ever want to go back there." Her body went limp and her eyes closed again. "We're gonna sell it…"

"All right, Maddie. I won't take you there. Where do you want me to take you, to your parents?"

She stayed silent for a moment and he wondered if she was trying to decide. But then too much time went by. He glanced over and sighed. She had fallen asleep. Damn. The last thing he wanted to do was carry her into her parents' house drunk. They'd be appalled.

Which left only one option. He did a U-turn at the next light and headed back toward the freeway. It looked like she would be staying with him tonight after all.

Gabe managed to open the door to his house and carry Maddie inside. She was completely out, her head thrown back over his arm and her body a dead weight in his grasp.

He kicked the door closed behind him and carried her to his spare bedroom. After laying her down on the bed, he pulled off her one shoe, and then removed the rest of her clothing. The lingerie she had on underneath made him pause.

It was the same bra and panty set that he'd seen hanging in her bathroom that first time he went to her apartment.

"Maddie," he murmured, sitting on the edge of the bed and stroking a piece of hair off her face. "Why can't I think straight when you're near me?"

"Mmm." She groaned and muttered, "I can't stop thinking about it. I killed him. I killed a man."

Gabe drew back, not realizing she'd woken up. Her eyes were still closed, and she might've been talking to herself in her sleep. Or in her drunken state. His gut twisted with sympathy.

"It was you or him, Maddie," he murmured, trying to soothe her. "You had no choice. You've got to stop thinking about it."

She sat up and crawled forward until she was beside him, then dropped her head on his thigh and lay back down.

"Maybe." She sighed. "I just keep seeing him. Seeing him dead on the stairs. Have you ever killed someone?"

His thoughts immediately went to Ricky. Two weeks ago he would've said yes to her question. But that night on Whidbey had changed him. She had changed him.

"No," he answered finally, stroking her hair. "But in my line of work, it's always a possibility."

"I hope you don't have to. It really sucks."

"I'm sure it does."

After a while she fell asleep again and he eased her back onto the mattress. After pulling the sheets up over her, he turned off the lamp and left the room.

Gabe woke the moment she entered his room. Always a light sleeper, he'd known she was there before she could even climb into his bed.

Maddie scooted close to him and then her mouth was on his naked chest as her hand reached down to grab his cock.

Gabe groaned and reached for her hand, stilling it. He glanced at the time and realized it had only been an hour. She was still drunk, and probably just horny.

"Go back to bed, Maddie," he ordered, trying to ease her away from him.

"No. I don't want to." She climbed on top of him, straddling his hips.

"No." He reached up to grasp her waist, fully intending to lift her off him.

"Come on, Gabe." She slid back until her ass came in contact with his erection. She wiggled against him until his cock reared upwards. "I need you."

Gabe's mouth went dry when she unfastened her bra and slid it off. Her full breasts swung loose, the nipples already hard.

"Suck on them," she whispered, leaning forward until her breasts were in his face.

He couldn't have resisted for anything. Reaching up, he squeezed her breasts, pulling them toward him until he could cover one of her nipples with his mouth. His teeth closed over the firm tip and she moaned when he tugged gently.

He slipped a hand down her stomach until he reached her panties. Wiggling his fingers underneath the lace, he immediately sought the hot wetness of her center.

"God, yes!" Madison groaned and clenched around his fingers. "I've missed this."

He kept sucking her nipple while he drove his fingers deeper into her, in and out, until her scent permeated the air and his fingers were slick with her desire.

"Please, I need you inside me. Not just your fingers."

Her hand wrapped around his erection, guiding it between her thighs.

Needing no more encouragement, he caught her wrists and pressed them to the bed, then slowly slid inside her.

Her guttural groan matched his. Inch by inch he sank into her. God he'd missed this, missed her. He thrust faster and she lifted her hips, bringing him deeper.

They moved in rhythm—one they'd established in their time together.

And then he knew he wouldn't last much longer. He'd

missed her too much, missed being inside her.

"Maddie." He groaned and reached between them to rub her clit while he emptied himself inside her.

Another pregnancy scare? The thought passed through his head briefly. God, they could never be the poster children for safe sex.

Gabe closed his eyes and slowly pulled out of her. He lay down beside her, pressing a kiss onto her shoulder.

"I'm glad you came to me tonight." He ran a hand down her naked back.

She didn't answer and he realized she'd fallen asleep. Gabe closed his eyes, hoping this meant she'd forgiven him.

Chapter Twenty-Four

Madison woke with a pounding headache, nausea, and cottonmouth. She debated which one to take care of first and then it hit her. She was at Gabe's house. She just couldn't remember how she'd gotten here.

In fact there wasn't a lot she remembered from the previous evening. Had they had sex? Several images flitted through her head but were gone as quickly as they'd come.

"And this is why I never drink," she muttered, pressing a hand against her throbbing head.

She looked at her watch and frowned. Hmm, it was nine-thirty. There was something she had to do at noon.

Shoot! The wedding!

Madison threw the covers off and grabbed her clothes, pulling them on. The soreness in various parts of her body made her think that they had indeed gotten it on. Jesus, had she told him she loved him in the midst of an orgasm? It wouldn't surprise her.

"Gabe," she screamed, hobbling around his house. "*Gabe.* Where are you?"

She found a note taped to the fridge—she knew now that he was big on leaving notes there—and sighed in frustration. He'd gone for a run. It must be nice to be a guy. Maybe he could get ready for a wedding in a half-hour, but she needed at least two hours.

She picked up the phone and called for a taxi. By the time it had arrived, Gabe still hadn't returned. During the ride to her car, she wondered again what had happened between them last night. Had she spilled her guts and confessed her second thoughts? Or maybe just torn off his clothes and had wild drunken sex? Hmm.

Once home, Madison managed to get dressed, do her hair, and arrive at the hotel by eleven. A freaking miracle if she did say so herself. And, thankfully, the painkillers were kicking in for her headache. Now, if only she'd had a chance to eat something.

"Madison!" Christy came running up to her. "Do you have anything blue on you? Lannie forgot something blue and she's about to have a breakdown soon if she doesn't find something."

Madison shrugged and gave her a blank look. "I doubt it. Oh, wait, maybe in my car. I have one of those rubber bracelets that raise money for cancer. It's blue. Do you think she'd want to wear that?"

"Lord, you are a riot." Christy laughed, managing to look both innocent and gorgeous. It wasn't a mystery what Gabe saw in her. He'd be crazy not to want Christy.

Depressed at the sudden thought, Madison looked away. She almost wished that she had told Gabe last night how she felt about him. That she'd made a mistake about them. Then at least she might have a chance.

Seeing him standing alone in the hallway a few minutes later, she approached him hesitantly.

"Hey, how are you feeling?" he asked, giving her a quick glance.

"All right." She moistened her lips with her tongue. "Umm,

about last night. I..."

His gaze grew unreadable and his jaw clenched. "It never should have happened?"

She swallowed hard and hesitated. Was he telling her that, or assuming that's what she thought? "Last night is kind of hazy. I just want to know what happened and if I...said anything."

"Kind of hazy, Maddie?" He shook his head. "Is this the way you're playing it? You leave my house this morning while I'm out running so you don't have to see me. You don't even leave a note or make a phone call. I can take a hint, Maddie. It never happened. Done."

Madison flinched as he walked away. God, he *hated* her. He could barely look at her.

She went into the bathroom to splash some water on her face and touch up her makeup. She could have used the designated bridal suite, where the women were scurrying around and giggling like they were on speed. She winced and shook her head, having very little desire to jump into the festivities.

She needed this moment to be alone. To talk herself into believing Gabe was still all wrong for her. Besides, he had taken her back to his place when he knew she was drunk. What kind of man would take advantage of a woman that way?

Madison stared at herself in the mirror; she looked pale. She put on a little more blush and a darker shade of lipstick, hoping it would make her look less dead.

Her gaze dropped to the dress she wore. At least Lannie had picked out gorgeous bridesmaid dresses. They were champagne-colored, the top in corset fashion and the bottom being mostly tulle that came down to the calf. It made her breasts look good and her legs seem longer.

"Madison?" The door to the bathroom peeked open and another bridesmaid popped in. "Are you in here? Lannie's giving out last-minute instructions so you need to come back."

"Okay, I'll be right there." Madison waited until the other girl had left before giving herself a reassuring glance in the mirror.

She would get through this day. She'd been through worse. And after the wedding, there'd be no reason to see Gabe anytime soon. That would be a good thing, wouldn't it?

On the way back to the bridal suite, she began to wonder.

"All right, ladies, listen up!"

Lannie could be heard from halfway down the halls of the building. Madison increased her pace as much as she could with her foot in a cast, and went to join them.

She lined up next to John and waited for the signal indicating it was their turn to walk down the aisle. Two couples had already gone and they were up after two more.

"You look good enough to eat, sweetheart," John whispered.

"Excuse me?" She gave him a sharp glance. She vaguely remembered hanging out with him at the rehearsal dinner. He'd been the one to bring her all those drinks.

"What do you say we go get a hotel room after the reception?" he asked. "I'll even pay."

"What in the hell makes you think I'd go to a hotel with you?"

"You almost did last night." He grabbed her arm as they finally got their signal to walk.

While they started their slow stroll down the aisle, more memories from last night flickered through Madison's head.

Dear God. Had she really almost gone home with this loser? What had stopped her? Or who?

Her gaze lifted to the front of the room where Gabe already stood next to Eric. Oh, God. Gabe hadn't taken advantage of her—he'd stopped John from doing it.

The rest of the events from last night slowly became clear in her mind, from her begging him not to take her home, to how he'd sat with her head on his lap, stroking her hair while she talked about the horror of killing another person. And then how she'd climbed into his bed and...

It all came back. They'd made love again. She'd begged him to.

Gabe's eyes suddenly met hers, and the look in them made the air lock in her throat. The raw emotion in his gaze remained for a few seconds before he once again schooled his expression into an unreadable mask.

But she had seen it. And she had responded. For a moment, she'd imagined what it would be like to walk down the aisle toward Gabe at her own wedding. To become Mrs. Martinez. She had sensed the complete rightness of it all. And she wanted it. She wanted him. So much it hurt. Oh God, but was it too late?

She took her place next to another bridesmaid and waited for the rest of the procession to take place. Soon Lannie was making the life-altering walk down the aisle toward Eric.

Madison swallowed hard as she saw the love in the other couple's eyes. She dropped her gaze and waited for the pastor to begin the ceremony.

When they came to the part where they recited their vows, Madison again looked at Gabe. He'd already been watching her and their gazes locked and held. Her pulse raced.

The sounds of applause snapped them both back to their

surroundings, and Madison blinked rapidly to get her emotions back under control.

Eric and Lannie walked back down the aisle with their hands clasped, full of smiles. Madison watched as Gabe and Christy linked arms and then followed the newlyweds.

A moment later John escorted her down the aisle and into the lobby where everyone seemed to be congregating.

She forced John's hand off her arm and stepped away from him, scanning the crowd for Gabe. She couldn't see him, and soon the mob of people shifted toward the reception area.

She found herself seated at a table with the bridal party on the opposite end from Gabe. Realizing she wouldn't be able to talk to him anytime soon, she tried to eat something. Although she'd been hungry earlier, she was much too nervous to eat now.

The sound of someone tapping their champagne glass filled the room, and everyone turned their focus to Gabe as he stood.

Madison knew that his glass held apple juice instead of champagne.

"I'd like to make a toast to the newlyweds," he began.

Madison's fingers tightened around her own glass of champagne, which she hadn't touched. Everything inside her ached as she stared at him.

"I've known Eric for about fifteen years," Gabe stated. "There's no one I respect or admire more. I didn't think there was a way for him to become a better person than he already was. But when Lannie came into his life, she proved me wrong."

There were many sighs throughout the room as Eric took Lannie's hand in his and they smiled at each other.

Gabe turned to face them and lifted his glass. "When you find someone who makes you a better person because you love them, then you've found gold. I envy you both. Here's to Eric and Lannie."

"To Eric and Lannie." The crowd echoed dutifully and drank from their glasses.

Madison dropped her gaze, not wanting anyone to see the sudden sheen of tears. She barely heard Christy give her toast next. She would do whatever it took to convince Gabe to give her another chance.

The trio of hired musicians began playing a slow jazz standard, and the newlyweds were called onto the floor for their first dance.

Madison looked around, trying to locate Gabe again. She spotted him standing near the back, like he might be considering leaving.

The thought sent her nerves into overdrive. If she didn't do it now, she never would. She waited until Eric and Lannie were center stage, before crossing the room toward him. She made it halfway there when he turned and left the hall, walking back into the lobby.

Madison hurried after him, hoping she would catch him before he could get out the door.

"Gabe!" she whisper-yelled but he didn't seem to hear her. She didn't want to yell any louder or she might distract from Eric and Lannie.

Thinking quick, she took the sandal off her good foot and chucked it at him, hoping her aim was true. It smacked him dead center in the back. He froze, turning slowly with an expression of disbelief on his face, which turned to wariness.

"Hi," she whispered as she hobbled toward him. "Can we talk?"

"Are you sure you want to talk? Or maybe you'd just like to

hit me with your other shoe."

"I don't have another shoe. I have a cast. And I didn't want to yell and divert the attention from the newlyweds," she said defensively. "But I had to get your attention somehow. I'm sorry. Did I hurt you?"

He raised an eyebrow, amusement flickering in his eyes now.

"I didn't think so." She looked around, trying to find a place for them to be alone and sit.

"You said you wanted to talk, Maddie?"

She nodded, not trusting herself to speak all of a sudden.

"Maddie?"

Before she could answer him, Lannie started speaking into the microphone in the reception room.

"I'd like to have the next dance be between my maid of honor and the best man. Will you both come forward?"

Madison scowled. *Damn Lannie and her matchmaking.*

"God, I don't want to dance." He groaned, not looking very pleased at the notion.

"Good, because you're not going to." She dragged him quickly around a corner to a small door, which she jerked open. "Hurry, we can hide in here."

Gabe ducked in first and she went in after him, shutting the door firmly behind her. Wherever they were, it was a pretty small area. She had to search a second before finding the metal chain hanging from the ceiling. Madison tugged on it and the light came on. They both looked around at their surroundings.

"Nice. A broom closet," Gabe murmured, his lips curving into a half-smile. "Are we going to do something dirty in here?"

"We could."

His expression turned serious, as if he hadn't expected her to take his teasing seriously.

"Maddie, I can't do this anymore. I'm not looking to be your fling of convenience. You said some pretty final things on Sunday—"

"I said terrible things." She swallowed hard. "Horrible things that I didn't mean."

"Well, you seemed eager to block last night out of your head, too."

"I had too much to drink and it was kind of hazy. But I remember now, and I don't regret it. Any of it. I'm so sorry, Gabe." She started crying. "I'm so, so sorry. I never expected perfection from you, despite how it may have seemed. And I never should have blamed you for what happened."

"Maddie." Relief flared in his gaze. He groaned as he pulled her close to him. "Sweet Maddie, you don't have to say anymore."

"No, but I do," she insisted between her tears. "I have to say that it wasn't just lust and hero worship—although you are my hero, Gabe. I know that you would have never intentionally put me in danger."

"Oh, *mi vida.*" He used his thumbs to stroke the tears from her cheeks.

"I was wrong, Gabe. Can you ever forgive me?"

"You know I do. And you know I would have given anything to have been there that day," he told her vehemently. "To make sure you didn't have to go through that."

"Yes, I do. I really do, Gabe. I just wish I could have acknowledged it sooner." She grasped his wrists. "I still have one more thing to say."

"Don't, Maddie. It's in the past—"

"I think I'm in love with you."

His thumbs stilled and his hands, which were cupping her face, tightened slightly.

"Gabe?" She looked up at him with sudden dread. Maybe it was too late. Maybe they could forgive each other, but that would be as far as it could go.

Her fear evaporated when he lowered his head to hers and covered her mouth with his own, his tongue moving between her lips to slip deep inside. Madison gave something between a sigh of relief and a laugh as she wound her arms around his neck.

"The feeling is mutual, *mi vida*," he finally whispered against her mouth as backed her up against the door.

Gabe shoved the fluffy dress up around her waist while she went to work freeing him from his tuxedo pants.

"I'm on birth control now," she murmured as he pulled her nylons off, followed by her panties. "Have been for a bit."

"Good." He plunged two fingers between her legs and inside her.

"Oh God." Her knees went weak as he moved his fingers in and out. She could hear her own wetness and it made her hotter.

Gabe lifted her up and she wrapped her legs around his waist. A second later he thrust into her and Madison's body clenched around his thick erection.

Footsteps sounded in the hall and then came voices nearby. Gabe froze, buried to the hilt inside her with his fingers digging into her ass cheeks.

Madison bit her lip to keep quiet and ducked her head against his shoulder.

"I don't know where he could have gone!" Lannie's

exasperated voice came from right outside the door. "And Madison's disappeared, too."

Gabe rotated his hips, moving deeper and making Madison's mouth open on a silent gasp.

"I'm sure they're fine." Christy's voice sounded a bit weary and hinted that she knew more than Lannie did. "I'm not up for dancing right now anyway. Come on. Let's just go back to the reception. We can skip to the father-daughter dance."

"All right," Lannie muttered. "But this is really weird. You would think they'd be in the other room waiting…"

Their voices drifted away and Madison let out the groan she'd been suppressing.

"That was close." Gabe pulled out a bit and then thrust back in hard, making her jerk against the wall.

"Should we hurry and go back out?"

"Do you really want to go and socialize with a bunch of stuffy old people?" he asked, nuzzling her neck.

"You're right. Let's stay in here and keep doing the sex thing." She tilted his chin so he looked up at her. "I love you, Gabriel Martinez."

She watched the flicker of possessiveness in his gaze and, as it settled into something deeper, her throat tightened with emotion.

He shook his head. "God, I love you so much, Maddie."

She gave him a watery smile and lowered her mouth to his again.

About the Author

To learn more about Shelli Stevens, please visit www.shellistevens.com. Send an email to Shelli at shellistevens@aol.com or join her Yahoo! group to join in the fun with other readers as well as Shelli! http://groups.yahoo.com/group/shellistevens

When a member of the CIA's premiere counter-terrorism unit
discovers the woman he loves is a suspected terrorist
he'll go to any lengths to uncover the truth.

Long Road Home
© 2007 Sharon Long

Jules Trehan disappeared without a trace three years ago much to the dismay of her parents and Manuel Ramirez. A counter terrorism specialist, Manny has utilized every agency resource in his attempt to discover what happened to Jules, to no avail.

As suddenly as she disappeared, Jules reappears in a small Colorado town. Injured in an explosion, she's hospitalized, and Manny rushes to her side, determined not to ever let her go again.

But Jules has one last job to do or Manny's life will be forfeit. A mission she must complete, even if it means betraying the only man she's ever loved.

Available now in ebook and print from Samhain Publishing.

Enjoy the following excerpt from Long Road Home…

Jules stared out her window, the miles passing in a blur. To Manny she probably appeared as though she were resting, unaware of where they were going, but she was paying attention to every detail of the landscape.

She hadn't seen a sign in miles, but the location of the sinking sun told her they were headed south and slightly east. Likely into New Mexico or West Texas.

"If you want to know where we're going, all you have to do is ask," Manny said dryly.

She twisted in her seat, surprised once again at his perception. "Where are we going?"

"New Mexico." He didn't offer more and didn't look over at her though she was staring hard at him.

She sank lower in the seat, gingerly drawing her knees up to her chest. Her fingers stroked the duffle bag at her side, drawing assurance from the outline of the gun there. If anyone found her and Manny, at least she'd have a way to defend them.

A sharp pain twisted through her chest and robbed her of breath. She sucked in air, determined not to panic as the scenery blurred before her. Damn, her ribs were on fire. She reclined the seat in an attempt to alleviate the growing pressure in her midsection.

The pain eased as she stretched out, and her breathing evened. She pressed her hands to her temples and squeezed her eyes shut, the thudding of her pulse pounding incessantly against her fingertips.

"Speak to me, Jules. What's wrong? Do I need to get you back to the hospital?" Manny's concerned voice seared through her haze of pain.

"No," she said faintly. "I'm all right. Really."

"Where are you, baby? Because you're miles away from here right now."

She cringed, not wanting to voice what she had been thinking. It sounded pathetic and defeatist. But she blurted it out anyway. "I was thinking it should have been me who died. Not Mom and Pop."

To her surprise, he slammed on the brakes and pulled over to the shoulder. He turned on her, his eyes blazing in the faint light offered by the headlights. "Don't say that. Don't ever say that," he said fiercely. "I thought I lost you, Jules. For three long years I lived with the awful reality you might not be coming home. And then I found you. Don't you dare wish you had died, because I've spent the last three years praying you were alive."

Before she could respond, he put his hand around the back of her neck and pulled her to meet his lips. Her mouth opened in surprise, and his tongue darted forward, gently probing her lips.

It was everything she had ever dreamed it would be. For a moment, she was in high school again, dressing for the prom, depressed because the one guy she wanted to take was eight years older and already out of college. She had closed her eyes and imagined it was Manny kissing her when her date had delivered her to the door with the prerequisite peck on the lips.

He was exquisitely gentle, his lips moving so softly across hers, reverently almost. His fingers worked slowly into her hair, kneading and stroking as he deepened his kiss.

Then, as suddenly as it had begun, it ended. He pulled quickly away from her and ran a hand through his hair in agitation. "Christ, I'm sorry, Jules. You don't need that right now."

She stared at him in shock. With a trembling hand, she raised her fingers and touched her slightly swollen lips.

"Don't look at me like that," he pleaded. He captured her hand and brought it to his lips, kissing it softly. "I'm sorry, baby."

He allowed her hand to slide from his, and she took it back, cradling it with her other hand. What was she supposed to say? She was so damn confused, she doubted she could recall her own name at the moment. For that matter, she really had no idea what her real name was. A hysterical bubble of laughter rose quickly in her throat, and she fought to choke it back.

Manny swore softly then pulled back onto the highway. "Get some sleep, Jules. If you don't, I swear, I'll call Tony and have you transferred to the hospital we'd planned. It's what I should've done in the first place."

"Who the hell is Tony anyway?" she grumbled as she lay back against the leather seat. She shivered slightly, and Manny reached over to turn up the heat.

"Tony is my partner."

"Partner in what? Somehow I doubt you're still in the computer software business." He looked far too dangerous to be a computer nerd. She had never been able to reconcile his image with his profession.

"Rest," he said in a warning tone. "We'll talk when we get there."

"Wherever there is," she said in exasperation.

He smiled.

"What's so funny?"

"You are. You're sounding more and more like the Jules I know all the time."

She sobered instantly, the throbbing in her head resuming

with a vengeance. "I'm not her," she said softly. "Maybe I never was."

Manny remained silent, his hands gripping the steering wheel tighter. "Rest."

Not arguing, she turned to the window. She could never go back to that carefree, naïve girl she had once been. She'd seen and done far too much. In a faint moment of shame, she was glad Mom and Pop never got to see the person she'd become. Their disappointment would have been more than she could bear.

She raised trembling fingers to her lips, lips still swollen from Manny's kiss. What exactly were his feelings for her? She'd never imagined that he returned her sentiment, that he might want her just as badly as she'd wanted him, but in the face of the way he'd kissed her, she could hardly ignore the possibility. Had she been blind to the signs?

She thought back, trying to analyze Manny's behavior toward her. As a teenager, she'd idolized him, fantasized about being Mrs. Manuel Ramirez, but she'd been careful to keep her girlish imaginings to herself. She would have died if he'd found out the extent of her infatuation.

Three years ago, she would have done anything for Manny to kiss her like he just had, but now it only complicated matters. No matter how much she wanted him to be more than a big brother protective figure, it wasn't possible. And if he knew the truth about her, he wouldn't want her anyway.

"It's snowing." He turned to her when she looked over. "You used to love the snow."

"Yeah," she said faintly. But she didn't now. It was too easy to be tracked in the snow. She remained silent, not voicing that tidbit of information. Instead she watched the flurry of snowflakes through the windshield wipers.

The heat pouring from the vents and the steady hum of the wipers lulled her into a state of relaxation. Soon her eyes grew as heavy as her heart, and she allowed them to close. Her final thought was that she hoped it wasn't snowing wherever they ended up.

hot stuff

Discover Samhain!

THE HOTTEST NEW PUBLISHER ON THE PLANET

Romance, fantasy, mystery, thriller, mainstream and
more—Samhain has more selection, hotter authors, and
everything's available in both ebook and print.

Pick your favorite, sit back, and enjoy the ride!
Hot stuff indeed.

GET IT NOW

MyBookStoreAndMore.com

GREAT EBOOKS, GREAT DEALS . . . AND MORE!

Don't wait to run to the bookstore down the street, or
waste time shopping online at one of the "big boys." Now,
all your favorite Samhain authors are all in one place—at
MyBookStoreAndMore.com. Stop by today and discover
great deals on Samhain—and a whole lot more!

Samhain
publishing LTD

WWW.SAMHAINPUBLISHING.COM